William Harrison Ainsworth

Ballads, Romantic, Fantastical, and Humorous

William Harrison Ainsworth

Ballads, Romantic, Fantastical, and Humorous

ISBN/EAN: 9783744784528

Printed in Europe, USA, Canada, Australia, Japan

Cover: Foto ©Andreas Hilbeck / pixelio.de

More available books at **www.hansebooks.com**

ROMANTIC, FANTASTICAL, AND HUMOROUS,

TO WHICH IS ADDED

COMBAT OF THE THIRTY.

MPRISING A NEW CHAPTER OF FROISSART.

BY

WILLIAM HARRISON AINSWORTH.

Illustrated by Sir John Gilbert, J.R.A.

LONDON:

GEORGE ROUTLEDGE AND SONS,

THE BROADWAY, LUDGATE.

NEW YORK: 416, BROOME STREET.

CONTENTS.

Legendary and Romantic Ballads.

Fantastical Ballads.

Humorous Ballads.

Translations.

The Combat of the Thirty.

ILLUSTRATIONS.

William Harrison Ainsworth was born in King Street, Manchester, at the house of his father, who was a solicitor of high standing and extensive practice, on the 4th February, 1805. His paternal grandfather, Jeremiah Ainsworth, one of the founders of the Lancashire School of Geometry, has already been noticed (vol. ii. p. 48). By the side of his mother, Ann, the daughter of the Rev. Ralph Harrison, he was descended from a line of Nonconformists, some of whom Calamy has embalmed in his pages. William Harrison, who was gifted by nature with a fine constitution, high spirits, and a most joyous temperament, after receiving elementary tuition from his uncle, the Rev. William Harrison, who held a highly respectable rank as a teacher, became on the 20th March, 1817, a scholar of the Manchester Free Grammar School, where he remained for some years. A vivid sketch, in which he has brought the school and its masters with such life and spirit before us, appears in *Mervyn Clitheroe.* At the annual recitations he appeared to great advantage, and his remarkably handsome face, excellent delivery and perfect self-possession are still recollected by the surviving attenders of those interesting occasions, and never failed to bring down plaudits from the audience. Of Dr.

Smith he was always a great favourite, and that sagacious master well understood that he was no common boy. While at school and afterwards he went through a large amount of miscellaneous reading, in which, besides recourse to his father's collection, which was a good one, he had the advantage, a benefit which Thomas de Quincey had availed himself of before him, of the old Exchange Circulating Library, now broken up and dispersed, in which there was an ample if not select table provided with dishes of all sorts, from *Amadis of Gaul* and *Palmerin of England* to Bryant's *Mythology*, and Cudworth's *Intellectual System*. On leaving the Free Grammar School he was placed by his father with Mr. Alexander Kay, an able and experienced solicitor, afterwards Mayor of Manchester, with a view to his succeeding to the well-established business which his father carried on in partnership with his son's early and intimate friend, the present president of the Chetham Society.

Mr. Thomas Ainsworth, the father, to whose energy and public spirit the improvements in Manchester were materially indebted, died at a comparatively speaking early age, in 1824. His son, William Harrison, went through the regular legal curriculum, and from Mr. Kay's office in Manchester proceeded to Mr. Jacob

Phillips's chambers in King's Bench Walks to be perfected in the higher mysteries of conveyancing. Here he copied precedents, and we have a folio volume in which his labours are embodied, but the rule in Shelley's case and Fearne's contingent remainders had no charms for him. His aspirations were of another kind—to give new associations to the name of Ainsworth unconnected with Law, Mathematics or Lexicography—in short, to enter upon a literary career; and to know and be known by the leading authors of the day, exchanging Manchester with all its prospects for the great metropolis. In this resolve he was confirmed by marrying (October, 1826) Ann Frances, the beautiful daughter of Mr. John Ebers, of Old Bond Street, the lessee of the Opera House, whose London connexions were large and extensive; and he accordingly became settled in the midst of the world of letters and fashion. For some time he carried on the business of a publisher, and several works of interest and value may be found with his name attached; but this, after giving it a full and fair trial, he thought fit for wise reasons to discontinue; having, however, acquired an experience from his publishing operations which was afterwards undoubtedly beneficial to him. During all this period—at school, while going through his professional education in Manchester and London, and the years which immediately followed—he devoted the greater part of his leisure to contributing, sometimes solely, sometimes with a friendly collaborateur, to various periodicals; commencing with Arliss's little but elegantly illustrated magazine, and proceeding onward to those of larger size and greater pretensions. But, leaving these prolusions, as well as the separate works in poetry and prose, of what we may style the præ-Rookwoodian Era, to be indicated and enumerated by his future biographer—and biography has nothing more interesting than the examination of the early works of successful writers—we must come to the production which first gave Mr. Ainsworth a solid footing as an author. This was the striking, and in many respects unequal, story of *Rookwood*, but in which was contained what was at once acknowledged to be a masterpiece of descriptive power; we need not add that we refer to Turpin's celebrated Ride to York, which at once, delighting the young and the old, established the writer as a favourite of the reading public. *Rookwood* was followed by *Crichton*, which sustained, if it did not increase, the reputation Mr. Ainsworth had acquired. Most of the works which succeeded appeared originally in a serial form either in *Bentley's Miscellany*,

Ainsworth's Magazine, the *Sunday Times*, or in monthly numbers, and were afterwards collected into volumes. The first of these was the wonderfully popular and much calumniated *Jack Sheppard*, which, admirably illustrated by George Cruikshank, was universally read; and, by its extraordinary success, called forth attacks on all sides, and a spirit which, to lovers of fair play, looked very much like persecution. On this subject, we cannot do better than refer to Laman Blanchard's very sensible remarks in his *Memoir*.

The storm which *Jack Sheppard* had evoked was in a great measure appeased by the *Tower of London*, which deals with a higher class of criminals, and must always be placed amongst the best, if it be not indeed the best of the author's historical novels. During the last thirty years it has certainly lost none of its original popularity. Its great success gave occasion to a large dinner, which we well remember, in which were present, by Mr. Ainsworth's invitation, the leading authors, critics, artists, and publishers of London, and at which Serjeant (afterwards) Judge Talfourd presided. We doubt much whether, amongst the many similar celebrations which have since occurred in London, there has been any which went off more brilliantly, or with which the author, in compliment of whom the gathering took place, had better reason to be satisfied. The narrow limits of this notice necessarily prevent more than a simple enumeration of the titles of the novels which Mr. Ainsworth's creative power and extraordinary fertility have produced, from the date of *Rookwood* (1834) to the present time. One of them we must not, however, omit to single out from the rest—*Mervyn Clitheroe*—as it gives many graphic sketches of the friends and scenes with which he was familiar in boyhood. Another, *The Lancashire Witches*, dedicated to his old friend, the President of the Chetham Society, in which, with great artistic skill, he has worked up the materials contained in two works in the Chetham series of very different character—Potts's *Discovery* and *Nicolas Assheton's Journal*—will always have a peculiar interest as a powerful and striking delineation of the grand superstition of his native county. Nor should it be omitted that to the very pleasing story, the *Flitch of Bacon*, we owe, under the auspices of Mr. Ainsworth, the temporary revival of one of the most curious and interesting of the old customs of England, the giving of the flitch at Great Dunmow. We proceed to the list :—

Rookwood, 1834.

Crichton, 1837.

Jack Sheppard, 1839.

Tower of London, 1840.

Guy Fawkes, 1841.

Old St. Paul's, 1841.

The Miser's Daughter, 1842.

Windsor Castle, 1843.

*St. James's, or the Court of
    Queen Anne*, 1844.

Lancashire Witches, 1848.

Star-Chamber, 1854.

Flitch of Bacon, 1854.

Spendthrift, 1856.

Mervyn Clitheroe, 1857.

Ovingdean Grange, 1860.

Constable of the Tower, 1861.

Lord Mayor of London, 1862.

Cardinal Pole, 1863.

John Law the Projector, 1864.

*The Spanish Match, or Charles
    Stuart in Madrid*, 1865.

Myddleton Pomfret, 1865.

The Constable de Bourbon, 1866.

Old Court, 1867.

The South Sea Bubble, 1868.

Hilary St. Ives, 1869.

Talbot Harland, 1870.

Tower Hill, 1871.

Boscobel, 1872.

That in so long a series, and dealing with scenes and periods and subjects so diversified, Mr. Ainsworth should still have retained his hold upon public favour, as is sufficiently evidenced by the continually repeated impressions of his works both here, on the Continent, in America, and our colonial dependencies, and the translations of them into most of the languages of Europe, is an ample proof that he possesses those sterling qualities, as a writer of fiction, which will insure permanence to his name as an author. To continue to please the public by successive productions during a period of nearly forty years is a distinction accorded to few.

We must not forget to notice the collection of Mr. Ainsworth's ballads, published in 1855, which makes us regret that he has not continued to cultivate a species of composition for which he seems to have a peculiar talent. Nor can we pass by *The Combat of the Thirty, from an old Breton Lay of the* 14*th Century*, 1859, 8vo, a most spirited and excellent version which we should be glad to see in an illustrated form, which is all that is needed to give it an extensive popularity.

Mr. John Forster, in the first volume of his *Life of Charles Dickens,* has referred with evident pleasure to the kindly intercourse which existed between the far-famed Boz, himself, and Mr. Ainsworth, in the days gone by. We believe there is no one connected with literature, who has been brought within the range of the genial sympathy, the considerate feeling, and hearty and liberal hospitality of the subject of this notice, who will not have equal pleasure in looking back to the occasions when they met. We are sure there are no reminiscences that dwell more agreeably on our minds than of the days when Kensal Manor House, on the Harrow Road, where Mr. Ainsworth resided for many years, was a central point for literary men ; and when, after sitting under an admirable host and enjoying the conversation of men whom it was always a delight to meet, the guests were serenaded on those fine summer evenings as they went homewards by the nightingales which had not then deserted that part of the suburbs of London.   From Kensal Manor House Mr. Ainsworth removed to Brighton, and thence to Tunbridge Wells, but now resides with his eldest daughter at Hurstpierpoint.   He has likewise a residence at Reigate.

Mr. Ainsworth is a widower, his wife, Anne Frances, having died on the 6th March, 1838, leaving three daughters now living : 1, Fanny ; 2, Emily Mary ; 3, Blanche, married to Major Swanson, Royal Artillery.   His mother, Mrs. Ann Ainsworth, who inherited all the business talents of her father, the Rev. Ralph Harrison, one of those prescient spirits who looked forward to the immense growth of Manchester, died in March, 1842.

One of the advantages of the eminent authors of the present day is the admirable manner in which, as a rule, they have been represented pictorially. The portraits of Pickersgill and Maclise will always give, as far as painting can, to those unacquainted with the original, a perfect idea of the author of *Rookwood* when in the full bloom of age and authorship.

Mr. Ainsworth was present at the great banquet in October, 1871, commemorating the new erections of the Manchester Free Grammar School, the Earl of Derby presiding; and, in an interesting and very appropriate speech, from which, if our space had allowed, we should have wished to have given some extracts, took a review of the alumni, who in former days had done honour to the school.—*C.*

Legendary and Romantic Ballads.

Legendary and Romantic Ballads.

THE CUSTOM OF DUNMOW.

SHOWING HOW IT AROSE.

Fytte the First.

A Fond Couple make a Vow before the Good Prior of the Convent of our Lady of Dunmow, that they have loved each other well and truly for a Twelvemonth and a Day; and crave his Blessing.

I.

" WHAT seek ye here, my children dear?
   Why kneel ye down thus lowly
Upon the stones, beneath the porch
   Of this our Convent holy?"
The Prior old the pair bespoke
   In faltering speech, and slowly.

B 2

II.

Their modest garb would seem proclaim

The pair of low degree,

But though in cloth of frieze arrayed,

A stately youth was he:

While she, who knelt down by his side,

Was beautiful to see.

III.

" A Twelvemonth and a Day have fled

Since first we were united;

And from that hour," the young man said,

" No change our hopes has blighted.

Fond faith with fonder faith we've paid,

And love with love requited.

IV.

" True to each other have we been;

No dearer object seeing,

Than each has in the other found;

In everything agreeing.

And every look, and word, and deed

That breed dissension fleeing.

v.

"All this we swear, and take in proof

Our Lady of Dunmow!

For She, who sits with saints above,

Well knows that it is so.

Attest our Vow, thou reverend man,

And bless us, ere we go!"

vi.

The Prior old stretch'd forth his hands:

"Heaven prosper ye!" quo' he;

"O'er such as ye, right gladly we

Say '*Benedicite!*'"

On this, the kneeling pair uprose—

Uprose full joyfully.

Fytte the Second.

The Good Prior merrily bestoweth a boon upon the Loving Couple;

and getteth a noble Recompence.

I.

Just then, pass'd by the Convent cook—

 And moved the young man's glee;

On his broad back a mighty Flitch

 Of Bacon brown bore he.

So heavy was the load, I wis,

 It scarce mote carried be.

II.

"Take ye that Flitch," the Prior cried,

 "Take it, fond pair, and go:

Fidelity like yours deserves

 The boon I now bestow.

Go, feast your friends, and think upon

 The Convent of Dunmow."

III.

" Good Prior," then the youth replied,

  "Thy gift to us is dear,

Not for its worth, but that it shows

  Thou deem'st our love sincere.

And in return broad lands I give—

  Broad lands thy Convent near;

Which shall to thee and thine produce

  A Thousand Marks a Year!

IV.

" But this Condition I annex,

  Or else the Grant's forsaken:

That whensoe'er a pair shall come,

  And take the Oath we've taken,

They shall from thee and thine receive

  A goodly Flitch of Bacon.

V.

" And thus from out a simple chance

  A usage good shall grow;

And our example of true love

    Be held up evermo':

While all who win the prize shall bless

    The Custom of Dunmow."

VI.

"Who art thou, son?" the Prior cried;

    His tones with wonder falter—

"Thou shouldst not jest with reverend men,

    Nor with their feelings palter."

"I jest not, Prior, for know in me

    Sir Reginald Fitzwalter.

VII.

"I now throw off my humble garb,

    As I what I am, confest;

The wealthiest I of wealthy men,

    Since with this treasure blest."

And as he spoke, Fitzwalter clasp'd

    His lady to his breast.

VIII.

" In peasant guise my love I won,

    Nor knew she whom she wedded;

In peasant cot our truth we tried,

    And no disunion dreaded.

Twelve months' assurance proves our faith

    On firmest base is steadied."

IX.

Joy reign'd within those Convent walls

    When the glad news was known;

Joy reign'd within Fitzwalter's halls

    When there his bride was shown.

No lady in the land such sweet

    Simplicity could own;

A natural grace had she, that all

    Art's graces far outshone:

Beauty and worth for want of birth

    Abundantly atone.

L'Envoy.

Hence the Custom.

What need of more?   That Loving Pair
   Lived long and truly so;
Nor ever disunited were;—
   For one death laid them low!
And hence arose that Custom old—
   The Custom of Dunmow.

THE LEGEND OF THE LIME TREE.

Amid the grove o'er-arched above with lime-trees old and tall,

(The avenue that leads unto the Rookwood's ancient hall),

High o'er the rest its towering crest one tree rears to the sky,

And wide out-flings, like mighty wings, its arms umbrageously.

Seven yards its base would scarce embrace—a goodly tree I
  ween,

With silver bark, and foliage dark of melancholy green;

And 'mid its boughs two ravens house, and build from year
  to year,

Their black brood hatch—their black brood watch—then scream-
  ing disappear.

In that old tree when playfully the summer breezes sigh,

Its leaves are stirred, and there is heard a low and plaintive cry;

And when in shrieks the storm blast speaks its reverend boughs

    among,

Sad wailing moans, like human groans, the concert harsh prolong.

But whether gale or calm prevail, or threatening cloud hath fled,

By hand of Fate, predestinate, a limb that tree will shed:

A verdant bough, untouched, I trow, by axe or tempest's breath,

To Rookwood's head an omen dread of fast-approaching death.

Some think that tree instinct must be with preternatural power,

Like 'larum bell Death's note to knell at Fate's appointed hour;

While some avow that on its bough are fearful traces seen,

Red as the stains from human veins commingling with the green.

Others, again, there are maintain that on the shattered bark

A print is made, where fiends have laid their scathing talons

    dark:

That, ere it falls, the raven calls thrice from that wizard bough;

And that each cry doth signify what space the Fates allow.

In olden days, the Legend says, as grim Sir Ranulph view'd

A wretched hag her footsteps drag beneath his lordly wood,

His blood-hounds twain he called amain, and straightway gave

    her chase :

Was never seen in forest green, so fierce, so fleet a race !

With eyes of flame to Ranulph came each red and ruthless

    hound,

While mangled, torn—a sight forlorn!—the hag lay on the

    ground.

E'en where she lay was turned the clay, and limb and reeking

    bone

Within the earth, with ribald mirth, by Ranulph grim were

    thrown.

And while as yet the soil was wet with that poor witch's gore,

A lime-tree stake did Ranulph take, and pierced her bosom's

    core.

And, strange to tell, what next befel !—that branch at once took

    root,

And richly fed, within its bed, strong suckers forth did shoot.

From year to year fresh boughs appear—it waxes huge in size;

And, with wild glee, this prodigy Sir Ranulph grim espies.

One day, when he, beneath that tree, reclined in health and pride,

A branch was found upon the ground—the next, Sir Ranulph

    died !

And from that hour a fatal power has ruled that Wizard Tree,

To Ranulph's line a warning sign of doom and destiny :

For when a bough is found, I trow, beneath its shade to lie,

Ere suns shall rise thrice in the skies a Rookwood sure shall

    die !

LEGEND OF THE LADY OF ROOKWOOD.

THE

LEGEND OF THE LADY OF ROOKWOOD.

GRIM Ranulph home hath at midnight come, from the long wars
of the Roses,

And the squire who waits at his ancient gates, a secret dark
discloses;

To that varlet's words no response accords his lord, but his
aspect stern

Grows ghastly white in the wan moonlight, and his eyes like the
gaunt wolf's burn.

To his lady's bower, at that lonesome hour, unannounced is Sir
Ranulph gone;

Through the dim corridor, through the hidden door, he glides—
she is all alone!

Full of holy zeal doth his young dame kneel at the meek
    Madonna's feet,
Her hands are pressed on her gentle breast, and upturned, is her
    visage sweet.

Beats Ranulph's heart with a joyful start, as he looks on her
    guiltless face;
And the raging fire of his jealous ire is subdued by the words of
    grace;
His own name shares her murmured prayers—more freely can
    he breathe;
But ah! that look! Why doth he pluck his poniard from its
    sheath?

On a footstool thrown lies a costly gown of saye and of minevere,
(A mantle fair for the dainty wear of a migniard cavalier),
And on it flung, to a bracelet hung, a picture meets his
    eye;—
" By my father's head," grim Ranulph said, " false wife, thy
    end draws nigh."

From off its chain hath the fierce knight ta'en that fond and

    fatal pledge;

His dark eyes blaze, no word he says, thrice gleams his dagger's

    edge!

Her blood it drinks, and, as she sinks, his victim hears his cry,

" For kiss impure of paramour, adult'ress, dost thou die!"

Silent he stood, with hands embrued in gore, and glance of flame,

As thus her plaint, in accents faint, made his ill-fated dame:

" Kind Heaven can tell, that all too well, I've loved thee, cruel

    lord;

But now with hate commensurate, assassin, thou'rt abhorred.

" I've loved thee long, through doubt and wrong; I've loved

    thee, and no other;

And my love was pure, for my paramour, as thou call'st him,

    was my brother!

The Red, Red Rose, on *thy* banner glows, on *his* pennon gleams

    the White,

And the bitter feud, that ye both have rued, forbids ye to unite.

c

"My bower he sought, what time he thought thy jealous vassals
    slept;
Of joy we dreamed, and never deemed that watch those vassals
    kept;
An hour flew by, too speedily!—that picture was his boon:
Ah! little thrift to me that gift: he left me all too soon!

"Wo worth the hour! dark fates did lower, when our hands
    were first united!
Fell lord, my truth, 'mid tears and ruth, with death hast thou
    requited:
In prayer sincere, full many a year of my wretched life I've
    spent;
But to hell's control would I give my soul, to work thy chastise-
    ment!"

These wild words said, low drooped her head, and Ranulph's
    life-blood froze,
For the earth did gape, as an awful shape from out its depths
    arose:

" Thy prayer is heard, Hell hath concurred," cried the Fiend,

   " thy soul is mine !

Like fate may dread each dame shall wed with Ranulph or his

   line !"

Within the tomb to await her doom is that hapless lady sleeping,

And another bride by Ranulph's side through the livelong night

   is weeping.

This dame declines—a third repines, and fades, like the rest,

   away :

Her lot she rues, whom a Rookwood woos—*cursed is her Wedding*

   Day!

CHARLES IX. AT MONTFAUCON.

I.

"To horse—to horse!" thus spake King Charles, "to horse, my
    lords, with me,

Unto Montfaucon will we ride—a sight you there shall see."

"Montfaucon, sire!" said his esquire—"what sight, my liege?
    how mean ye?"

"The carcase stark of the traitor dark, and heretic Coligni."

II.

The trumpets bray, their chargers neigh a loud and glad réveillé—

And plaudits ring, as the haughty king from the Louvre issues
    gaily;

On his right hand rides his mother, with her dames—a gorgeous
    train—

On his left careers his brother, with the proud Duke of Lorraine.

III.

Behind is seen his youthful Queen—the meek Elizabeth[1]—

With her damsels bright, whose talk is light of the sad, sad show

    of death :—

Ah, lovely ones!—ah, gentle ones! from the scoffer's judgment

    screen ye !—

Mock not the dust of the martyr'd just, for of such was good

    Coligni.

IV.

By foot uphung, to flesh-hook strung, is now revealed to all,

Mouldering and shrunk, the headless trunk of the brave old

    admiral;

[1] Elizabeth of Austria, daughter of the Emperor Maximilian, an amiable and excellent princess, whose genuine piety presented a striking contrast to the sanguinary fanaticism of her tyrannical and neglectful spouse. "O mon Dieu!" she cried, on the day of the massacre, of which she had been kept in ignorance; "quels conseillers sont ceux-là, qui ont donné le roi tel avis? Mon Dieu! je te supplie, et je requiers de lui pardonner, car si tu n'en as pitié, j'ai grand peur que cette offense ne lui soit pas pardonnée."

Gash-visaged Guise the sight doth please — fierce Lord, was
    naught between ye?

In felon blow of base Poltrot[1] no share had brave Coligni.

V.

"Now, by God's death!" the monarch saith, with inauspicious
    smile,

As, laughing, group the reckless troop round grey Montfaucon's
    pile;

"From off that hook its founder shook—Enguerrand de Marigni[2]—

But gibbet chain did ne'er sustain such burthen as Coligni."

[1] Jean Poltrot de Méré, the assassin of François de Guise, father of the
Balafré, probably in order to screen himself, accused Coligni and Beza of
being the instigators of his offence. Poltrot's flesh was afterwards torn from
his bones by red-hot pincers, but Henri of Lorraine never considered his
father's death fully avenged until the massacre of the Admiral. Coligni's
head was sent by Catherine de Medicis to Rome as an offering to Gregory
XIII. Upon this occasion the Pope had a medal struck off, stamped
with an exterminating angel, and subscribed—"Ugonotorum Strages."

[2] Pereat suâ arte Perillus. Enguerrand de Marigni, grand chamberlain
of France during the reign of Philippe-le-Bel, constructed the famous
gibbet of Montfaucon, and was himself among the first to glut its horrible
fourches patibulaires, whence originated the ancient adage—"Plus mal-
heureux que le bois dont on fait le gibet."

VI.

" Back! back! my liege," exclaimed a page, " with death the

    air is tainted,

The sun grows hot, and see you not, good sire, the queen has

    fainted ?"

" Let those retire," quoth Charles, in ire, " who think they stand

    too nigh;

To us no scent yields such content as a dead enemy."[1]

VII.

As thus he spake, the king did quake—he heard a dismal moan—

A wounded wretch had crept to stretch his bones beneath that

    stone :—

" Of dying man," groaned he, " the ban, the Lord's anointed

    dread,

My curse shall cling to thee, O king!—much righteous blood

    thou'st shed."

---

[1] Ensuite Coligni fut traîné aux fourches patibulaires de Montfaucon. Le Roi vint jouir de ce spectacle, et s'en montra insatiable. On ne concevait pas qu'il pût résister à une telle odeur; on le pressait de se retirer. Non, dit-il, le cadavre d'un ennemi sent toujours bon !—LACRATELLE.

VIII.

"Now by Christ's blood! by holy Rood!" cried Charles,
    impatiently;

"With sword and pike—strike, liegemen, strike!—God's death!
    this man shall die.

Straight halbert clash'd, and matchlock flash'd—but ere a shot
    was fired,

With laugh of scorn that wight forlorn had suddenly expired.

IX.

From the Louvre gate, with heart elate, King Charles that morn
    did ride;

With aspect dern did he return; quench'd was his glance of pride:

Remorse and ruth, with serpent tooth, thenceforth seized on his
    breast—

With bloody tide his couch was dyed—pale visions broke his rest![1]

[1] La maladie de Charles IX. était accompagnée de symptômes plus
violens qu'on n'en remarque dans les maladies de langueur; sa poitrine
était particulièrement affectée; mais son sang coulait par tous les pores;
d'affreux souvenirs persécutaient sa pensée dans un lit toujours baigné de
sang; il voulait et ne pouvait pas s'arracher de cette place.—LACRATELLE,
" Histoire de France pendant les Guerres de Religion."

YOLANDE.[1]

I.

A GOLDEN flower embroidering,

A lay of love low murmuring;

Secluded in the eastern tower

Sits fair Yolande within her bower:

    Fair—fair Yolande!

Suddenly a voice austere,

With sharp reproof breaks on her ear—

Her mother 'tis who silently

Has stolen upon her privacy—

    Ah! fair Yolande!

[1] A very free adaptation of a sparkling little romance by Audefroy le Bâtard, to be found in the Romancero François, entitled Bele Yolans. Much liberty has been taken with the concluding stanza—indeed, the song altogether bears but slight resemblance to its original.

" Mother! why that angry look?

Mother! why that sharp rebuke?

Is it that I while away

My solitude with amorous lay?

Or is it that my thread of gold

Idly I weave, that thus you scold

   Your own Yolande—Your own Yolande!"

II.

" It is not that you while away

Your solitude with amorous lay,

It is not that your thread of gold

Idly you weave, that thus I scold

         My fair Yolande!

Your want of caution 'tis I chide :—

The Baron fancies that you hide

Beneath the cushion on your knee

A letter from the Count Mahi :—

         Ah! fair Yolande!

Busy tongues have fill'd his brain

With jealousy and frantic pain;

Hither hastes he with his train!

And *if* a letter there should be

Conceal'd 'neath your embroidery,

Say no more.   But give it me,

   My own Yolande—My own Yolande!"

ESCLAIRMONDE.

[*Henri Trois sings at a Court Revel.*]

I.

THE crown is proud

    That decks our brow;

The laugh is loud—

    That glads us now.

The sounds that fall

    Around—above

Are laden all

    With love—with love—

        With love—with love.

II.

Heaven cannot show,

    'Mid all its sheen,

Orbs of such glow,

    As here are seen.

And monarch ne'er

   Exulting own'd,

Queen might compare

   With Esclairmonde—

      With Esclairmonde.

III.

From Bacchus' fount

   Deep draughts we drain;

Their spirits mount,

   And fire our brain;

But in our heart

   Of hearts enthroned,

From all apart

   Rests Esclairmonde—

      Rests Esclairmonde.

[*Chicot replies.*]

IV.

The crown is proud—

   But brings it peace?

The laugh is loud—

   Full soon 'twill cease.

The sounds that fall

   From lightest breath,

Are laden all

   With death—with death.

      With death—with death.

YUSEF AND ZORAYDA.[1]

I.

THROUGH the Vega of Granada, where the silver Darro glides—

From his tower within the Alpuxar—swift—swift Prince Yusef

    rides.

To her who holds his heart in thrall—a captive Christian maid—

On wings of fear and doubt he flies, of sore mischance afraid.

For ah! full well doth Yusef know with what relentless ire,

His love for one of adverse faith is noted by his sire:

" Zorayda mine!" he cries aloud—on—on—his courser strains—

" Zorayda mine!—thine Yusef comes!"—the Alhambra walls he

    gains.

[1] The incidents of this ballad are, with some slight variation, derived from those of the exquisite French romance, "Flore et Blancheflor," the date of which may be referred to the Thirteenth Century, and which unquestionably, as its recent editor, M. Paulin Paris, supposes, is of Spanish or Moorish origin.

II.

Through the marble court of Lions—through the stately
    Tocador—

To Lindaraxa's bowers he goes—the Queen he stands before;

Her maidens round his mother group—but not a word she
    speaks.

In vain amid that lovely throng, one lovelier form he seeks;

In vain he tries 'mid orient eyes, orbs darker far to meet;

No form so light, no eyes so bright, as hers his vision greet.

" Zorayda mine—Zorayda mine! ah whither art thou fled ?"

A low, low wail returns his cry—a wail as for the dead.

III.

No answer made his mother, but her hand gave to her son—

To the garden of the Generalif together are they gone;

Where gushing fountains cool the air—where scents the citron
    pale,

Where nightingales in concert fond rehearse their love-lorn tale,

Where roses link'd with myrtles make green woof against the
    sky,

Half hidden by their verdant screen a sepulchre doth lie;

" Zorayda mine — Zorayda mine ! — ah ! wherefore art thou

flown,

To gather flowers in Yemen's bowers while I am left alone !"

IV.

Upon the ground kneels Yusef—his heart is like to break;

In vain the Queen would comfort him—no comfort will he take,

His blinded gaze he turns upon that sculptured marble fair,

Embossed with gems, and glistening with coloured pebbles rare;

Red stones of Ind—black, vermeil, green, their mingled hues

combine,

With jacinth, sapphire, amethyst, and diamond of the mine.

" Zorayda mine—Zorayda mine !"—thus ran sad Yusef's cry,

" Zorayda mine, within this tomb, ah ! sweet one ! dost thou

lie ?"

V.

Upon that costly sepulchre, two radiant forms are seen;

In sparkling alabaster carved like crystal in its sheen;

The one as Yusef fashioned, a golden crescent bears,

The other, as Zorayda wrought, a silver crosslet wears,

And ever, as soft zephyr sighs, the pair his breath obey,

And meet within each other's arms like infants in their play.[1]

" Zorayda fair—Zorayda fair"—thus golden letters tell

A Christian maid lies buried here—by Moslem loved too well.

VI.

Three times those golden letters with grief sad Yusef reads,

To tears and frantic agony a fearful calm succeeds—

"Ah! woe is me; Zorayda mine—ah! would the self-same blow

That laid thee 'neath this mocking tomb, had laid thy lover low;

Two faithful hearts, like ours in vain stern death may strive to

    sever—

A moment more the pang is o'er, the grave unites us ever.

[1] This circumstance is thus depicted in the French romance:—

        En la tombe et quartre tuiaus
        Aus quartre cors bien fait et biaus.
        Es quiex li quartre vent féroient
        Chascuns, ainsi com'il ventoient.
        Quant li vens los enfans tochoit,
        L'un beisoit l'autre et accoloit;
        Si disoient, par nigromance
        De tout lor bon, de lor enfance.

                      FLORE ET BLANCHEFLOR.

Zorayda mine—Zorayda mine—this dagger sets me free—

Zorayda mine—look down—look down—thus—thus I come to

    thee !"

VII.

"Hold! Yusef, hold!" a voice exclaims, "thy loved Zorayda

    lives—

Thy constancy is well approved—thy sire his son forgives ;

Thine ardent passion doubting long—thy truth I thus have tried,

Behold her whom thy faith hath won—receive her as thy bride !"

In Yusef's arms—to Yusef's heart, Zorayda close is press'd,

Half stifled by a flood of joy, these words escape his breast :—

" Zorayda mine—Zorayda mine !—ah! doubly dear thou art ;

Uninterrupted bliss be ours, whom death has failed to part !"

THE LEGEND OF VALDEZ.[1]

I.

'Tis night!—forth Valdez, in disguise,

Hies;

And his visage, as he glides,

Hides.

Goes he to yon church to pray?

Eh!

No! that fane a secret path

Hath,

Leading to a neighbouring pile's

Aisles!

[1] Founded on a story in the "Hexameron" of Antonio de Torquemada, referred to in the amusing extravagancies of Monsieur Oufle. Subsequently to the publication of this lyric, the legend in question has been delightfully narrated by Washington Irving, in his "Spectral Researches in the Convent of San Francisco, at Seville, 1855."

Where nuns lurk—by priests cajoled

Old.

Thither doth Don Valdez go—

Oh!

Thither vestals lips to taste

Haste.

II.

'Neath you arch, why doth he stand?

And

Haps it that he lingers now

How?

Suddenly cowl'd priests appear

Here.

Voices chant a dirge-like dim

Hymn:

Mutes a sable coffin drear

Rear;

Where a monument doth lie

High.

'Scutcheons proud Death's dark parade

Aid.

Valdez sees, with fresh alarms,

Arms,

Which his own—(gules cross and star!)

Are.

III.

An hour—and yet he hath not gone

On!

Neither can he strength to speak

Eke.

" Hark!" he cries, in fear and doubt,

Out,

" Whom inter ye in that tomb?

Whom?—"

" Valdez!—He'll be, ere twelve hours,

Ours!—

Wait we for his funeral

All!"

IV.

" Monk ! thou bring'st, if this be truth,

Ruth !"

Valdez his own fate with dread

Read.

Question none he uttered more ;—

O'er

'Twas; and he doth peacefully

Lie

In the tomb he saw, thus crazed,

Raised.

L'Envoy.

MEMENTO MORI.   Life's a stale

Tale.

DITTY OF DU GUESCLIN.[1]

I.

A SILVER shield squire did wield, charged with an eagle black,

With talon red, and two-fold head, who followed on the track

Of the best knight that e'er in fight hurled mace, or couched the

    lance,

Du Guesclin named, who truncheon claimed as Constable of

    France.

---

[1] A free version of an "olde gentil" Breton lay of the age of Charles V. of France: a stanza is subjoined, that the reader may have a taste of it. The ballad, it may be observed, has remained wholly inedited, until the publication, by M. Crapelet, of the golden manuscript of the Combat des Trente, extracted from the Bibliothèque du Roi.

LE DISTIC DE MONS. BERTRAN DE GLASGUIN.

> Lescu dargent a . I . egle de sable
> A . ii. testes et . I . roge baston
> Pourtoist li preux le vallant connestable
> Qui de Glasguin Bertran auoist a nom

II.

In Brittany, where Rennes [1] doth lie, Du Guesclin first drew
breath ;

Born for emprise—in counsel wise, brave, loyal unto death.

With hand and sword, with heart and word, served well this
baron bold

The azure scutcheon that displayed three fleur-de-lis of gold. [2]

III.

Like Guesclin bold of warriors old in prowess there was
none,

'Mid peers that stood 'round Arthur good, Baldwin or brave
Bouillon :

Nor, as I ween, hath knighthood seen a chief more puissantly

With staff advance the flower of France 'gainst hostile chivalry.

A bron fu nes le chevalier Breton
Preux et hardi courageux come . I . tor
Qui tant serui de louial cuer et de bon
Lescu dazur a . iii . flours de lis dor.

[1] The Château de la Motte-Broon, near Rennes.

[2] The royal arms of France.

IV.

Guesclin is dead! and with him fled the bravest and the best,

That ever yet, by foe beset, maintained fair Gallia's crest!

His soul God shrive!—were he alive, his spear were couch'd again

To guard the three gold lilies from the white cross of Lorrain!"[1]

---

[1] The cognizance of the house of Guise. The double Cross of Lorrain was adopted as an ensign by the Leaguers, of whom the Duke of Guise was the prime mover: a circumstance which gave rise to the following sarcastic and somewhat irreverent quatrain, quite in the spirit of the times:—

> Mais, dites moi, que signifie
> Que les Ligueurs ont double croix?—
> C'est qu'en la Ligue on crucifie
> Jésus Christ encore une fois.

THE SWORD OF BAYARD.

THE SWORD OF BAYARD.

I.

"A boon I crave, my Bayard brave:"—'twas thus King Francis
spoke;

"The field is won, the battle done,[1] yet deal one other
stroke.

For by this light, to dub us knight, none worthy is as
thou,

Whom nor reproach nor fear approach, of prince or peer we
trow."

[1] The famous engagement with the Swiss, near Milan, in which Francis
the First came off victorious. Fleuranges places the ceremony of the
king's knighthood before the battle. The "Loyal Servant," however,
states that it occurred, as is most probable, after the conflict.

II.

"Sire!" said the knight, "you judge not right, who owns a
    kingdom fair,

'Neath his command all knights do stand—no service can he share."

"Nay! by our fay!" the king did say, "lo! at thy feet we kneel,

Let silken rules sway tiltyard schools, our laws are here of steel."

III.

With gracious mien did Bayard then his sword draw from his
    side;

"By God! St. Michael! and St. George! I dub thee knight!"
    he cried.

"Arise, good king! weal may this bring—such grace on thee
    confer,

As erst from blow of Charles did flow, Roland or Oliver!"

IV.

With belted blade, the king arrayed—the knight the spur applied,

And then his neck with chain did deck—and accolade supplied—

"Do thy devoir at ghostly choir—maintain high courtesie,

And from the fray in war's array, God grant thou never flee!"

V.

" Certes, good blade,"[1] then Bayard said, his own sword waving

 high,

" Thou shalt, perdie, as relic be preserved full carefully !

Right fortunate art thou, good sword, a king so brave to knight!

And with strong love, all arms above, rest honoured in my sight.

VI.

And never more, as heretofore, by Christian chivalry,

My trenchant blade shalt thou be rayed, or c'er endangered be !

For Paynim foes reserve thy blows—the Saracen and Moor

Thine edge shall smite in bitter fight, or merciless estour ! "[2]

VII.

Years, since that day, have rolled away, and Bayard hurt to

 death,

'Neath grey Rebecco's walls outstretched, exhales his latest

 breath.

[1] " Tu es bien heureuse d'avoir aujourd'hui, à un si beau et si puissant roi, donné l'ordre de chevalerie.   Certes, ma bonne épée, vous serez comme reliques gardée, et sur tout autre honoré !"—*Precis de la Chevalerie.*

 Estour—a grand mélee.

On Heaven he cried, or ere he died—but cross had none, I wist,

Save that good sword-hilt cruciform, which with pale lips he

    kissed.[1]

VIII.

Knight! whom reproach could ne'er approach, no name like unto

    thine,

With honour bright, unsullied, white, on Fame's proud scroll

    shall shine!

But were it not to mortal lot denied by grace divine,

Should Bayard's breath, and Bayard's death, and his good sword

    be mine.

[1] "This sword has been lost. Charles Emanuel, Duke of Savoy, requested it of Bayard's heirs. One of them, Charles du Motet, Lord of Chichiliane, sent him, in default of it, the battle-axe of which Bayard made use. The Duke told the Dauphinese gentleman, when he wrote to thank him for the present, 'That in the midst of the pleasure he felt at beholding this weapon placed in the worthiest part of his gallery, he could scarce choose but regret that it was not in such good hands as of its original owner.'"—CHAMPIER. See also the account of Bayard's death in the "Chronicle of the Loyal Servant."

THE SCOTTISH CAVALIER.

I.

From Scotia's clime to laughing France
  The peerless Crichton came;
Like him no knight could shiver lance,
  Wield sword, or worship dame.
Alas! each maiden sighs in vain,
  He turns a careless ear:
For queenly fetters fast enchain
  The Scottish cavalier!

II.

But not o'er camp and court, alone,
  Resistless Crichton rules;
Logicians next, defeated, own
  His empire o'er the Schools.

'Gainst sophists shrewd shall wit prevail,

Though tome on tome they rear;

And pedants pale, as victor, hail

The Scottish cavalier!

THE BLOOD-RED KNIGHT.

I.

SLOWLY unto the listed field I rode,

    Rouge was my charger's wide caparison;

And the same hue that on his housing glowed,

    Dyed, as with blood, my lance and morion.

II.

Rouge was my couvrechief, that swept the sward,

    Rouge the tall plume that nodded on my crest;

And the rich scarf—my loyalty's reward—

    Blushed, like a timorous virgin, on my breast.

III.

My broad ensanguined shield bore this device,

In golden letters writ, that all might see

How for bold deeds will lightest worth suffice ;

And thus it ran: " Les plus rouges y sont pris."

HYMN OF THE CONSPIRATORS IN THE GUNPOWDER PLOT.

I.

THE heretic and heathen, Lord,
Consume with fire, cut down with sword;
The spoilers from thy temples thrust,
Their altars trample in the dust.

II.

False princes and false priests lay low,
Their habitations fill with woe.
Scatter them, Lord, with sword and flame,
And bring them utterly to shame.

III.

Thy vengeful arm no longer stay,

Arise! O Lord, arise! and slay.

So shall thy fallen worship be

Restored to its prosperity!

DIRGE OF BOURBON.

I.

WHEN the good Count of Nassau
Saw Bourbon lie dead,
" By Saint Barbe and St. Nicholas!
Forward!" he said.

II.

" Mutter never prayer o'er him,
For litter ne'er halt;
But sound loud the trumpet—
Sound, sound to assault!

III.

" Bring engine—bring ladder,

Yon old walls to scale ;

All Rome, by Saint Peter !

For Bourbon shall wail."

ANACREONTIC ODE.[1]

I.

WHEN Bacchus' gift assails my brain,

Care flies, and all her gloomy train;

My pulses throb, my youth returns,

With its old fire my bosom burns;

Before my kindling vision rise

A thousand glorious phantasies!

Sudden my empty coffers swell

With riches inconsumable;

And mightier treasures 'round me spring

Than Crœsus owned, or Phrygia's king.

[1] Paraphrased from Ronsard's Ode—"Lorsque Bacchus entre chez noi," &c.

II.

Nought seek I in that frenzied hour,

Save love's intoxicating power;

An arm to guide me in the dance,

An eye to thrill me with its glance,

A lip impassioned words to breathe,

A hand my temples to enwreathe :

Rank, honour, wealth, and worldly weal,

Scornful, I crush beneath my heel.

III.

Then fill the chalice till it shine

Bright as a gem incarnadine !

Fill ! till its fumes have freed me wholly

From the black phantom—Melancholy !

Better inebriate 'tis to lie,

And dying live, than living die !

MARGUERITE DE VALOIS.[1]

I.

MARGUERITE, with early wiles—

Marguerite

On light Charins and D'Antragues smiles—[2]

Margot, Marguerite.

Older grown, she favours then,

Smooth Martigues,[3] and bluff Turenne.

The latter but a foolish pas,

Margot, Marguerite en bas.[4]

---

[1] A catalogue of Marguerite's various amourettes will be found in the "Divorce Satirique," published under the auspices of her consort, Henri IV. More than half, however, are, most probably, scandal.

[2] Marguerite was then of the tender age of eleven.

[3] Colonel-General of the French infantry. Brantôme has written his éloge.

[4] This refrain is attributed to the Duchess de Guise.

But no more these galliards please,

Marguerite.

Softly sues the gallant Guise,

Margot, Marguerite.

Guise succeeds, like God of war,

Valiant Henri of Navarre;

Better stop, than further go,

Margot, Marguerite en haut.

II.

Loudly next bewails La Mole,[1]

Marguerite,

On the block his head must roll,

Margot, Marguerite.

Soon consoles herself again,

With Brantôme, Bussi,[2] and Mayenne,[3]

Boon companion gros et gras,

Margot, Marguerite en bas.

---

[1] The Sieur La Mole, surnamed "Le Baladin de la Cour," beheaded by
Charles IX., it is said, from jealousy,—Mollis vita, Mollior interitus.

[2] Bussi D'Amboise.—Formosæ Veneris furiosi Martis alumnus.

[3] The Duc de Mayenne, brother to the Duc de Guise.

Who shall next your shrine adore,

Marguerite?

You have but one lover more,

Margot, Marguerite!

Crichton comes—the preux, the wise,

You may well your conquest prize;

Beyond him you cannot go,

Margot, Marguerite en haut.

THE ADMIRABLE CRICHTON.

A song I'll write on

Matchless Crichton;

In wit a bright one,

Form, a slight one,

Love, a light one!

Who talketh Greek with us

Like great Busbequius;

Knoweth the Cabala

Well as Mirandola;

Fate can reveal to us,

Like wise Cornelius;

Reasoneth like Socrates,

Or old Zenocrates;

Whose system ethical,

Sound, dialectical,

Aristotelian,

Pantagruelian,

Like to chameleon,

Choppeth and changeth.

Everywhere rangeth!

Who rides like Centaur,

Preaches like Mentor,

Drinks like Lyæus,

Sings like Tyrtæus,

Reads like Budæus,

Vaulteth like Tuccaro,

Painteth like Zucchero,

Diceth like Spaniard,

Danceth like galliard,

Tilts like Orlando,

Does all man can do!

" Qui pupas nobiles

Innumerabiles,

Amat amabiles ;

Atque Reginam

Navarræ divinam!"

Whose rare prosperity,

Grace and dexterity,

Courage, temerity,

Shall, for a verity,

Puzzle posterity.

THE THREE ORGIES.

I.

In banquet hall, beside the king,

Sat proud Thyestes revelling.

The festal board was covered fair,

The festal meats were rich and rare;

Thyestes ate full daintily,

Thyestes laughed full lustily;

But soon his haughty visage fell—

A dish was brought—and, wo to tell!

A gory head that charger bore!

An infant's look the features wore!

Thyestes shrieked—King Atreus smiled—

The father had devoured his child!

Fill the goblet—fill it high—

To Thyestes' revelry.

Of blood-red wines the brightest choose,

The glorious grape of Syracuse!

II.

For a victory obtained

O'er the savage Getæ chained,

In his grand Cæsarean hall

Domitian holds high festival.

To a solemn feast besought

Thither are the senate brought.

As he joins the stately crowd,

Smiles each pleased patrician proud,

One by one each guest is led

Where Domitian's feast is spread;

Each recoiling stares aghast

At the ominous repast;

Round marble slab of blackest shade

Black triclinia are laid,

Sable vases deck the board

With dark-coloured viands stored;

Shaped like tombs, on either hand,

Rows of dusky pillars stand;

O'er each pillar in a line,

Pale sepulchral lychni shine;

Cinerary urns are seen,

Graved each with a name, I ween,

By the sickly radiance shown

Every guest may read his own!

Forth then issue swarthy slaves,

Each a torch and dagger waves;

Some like Manes habited,

Figures ghastly as the dead!

Some as Lemures attired,

Larvæ some, with vengeance fired.

See, the throat of every guest

By a murderous gripe is prest!

While the wretch, with horror dumb,

Thinks his latest hour is come!

Loud then laugh'd Domitian,

Thus his solemn feast began.

Fill the goblet—fill it high—

To Domitian's revelry.

Let our glowing goblet be

Crown'd with wine of Sicily.

III.

Borgia[1] holds a papal fête,

And Zizime, with heart elate,

With his chiefs barbarian

Seeks the gorgeous Vatican.

'Tis a wondrous sight to see

In Christian hall that company !

[1] Pope Alexander VI., of the family of Lenzuoli, who assumed, previous to his pontificate, the name of Borgia, (a name rendered infamous,
as well by his own crimes and vices, as by those of the monster offspring,
Cæsar and Lucrezia, whom he had by the courtezan Vanozza,) according to
Gordon, was incited to the murder of Zizime or Djem, son of Mahomet II.,
by the offer of 300,000 ducats, from Bajazet, brother to the ill-fated
Othman Prince.

But the Othman warriors soon

Scout the precepts of Mahoun.

Wines of Sicily and Spain,

Joyously those paynims drain;

While Borgia's words their laughter stir,

"Bibimus Papaliter!"

At a signal, pages three,

With gold goblets, bend the knee;

Borgia pours the purple stream

Till beads upon its surface gleam.

"Do us a reason, noble guest,"

Thus Zizime, the pontiff pressed?

"By our triple-crown there lies

In that wine-cup Paradise!"

High Zizime the goblet raised—

Loud Zizime the Cyprus praised—

To each guest in order slow,

Next the felon pages go.

Each in turn the Cyprus quaffs,

Like Zizime each wildly laughs,—

Laughter horrible and strange!

Quick ensues a fearful change,

Stifled soon is every cry,

Azrael is standing by.

Glared Zizime—but spake no more:

Borgia's fatal feast was o'er!

   Fill the goblet—fill it high—

    With the wines of Italy;

    Borgia's words our laughter stir—

    Bibimus Papaliter!

ALL-SPICE, OR A SPICE OF ALL.

———

The people endure all,

The men-at-arms cure all,

The favourites sway all,

Their reverences flay all,

The citizens pay all,

Our good king affirms all,

The senate confirms all,

The chancellor seals all,

Queen Catherine conceals all,

Queen Louise instructs all,

Queen Margot conducts all,

The Leaguers contrive all,

The Jacobins shrive all,

The Lutherans doubt all,

The Zuinglians scout all,

The Jesuits flout all,

The Sorbonists rout all,

Brother Henri believes all,

Pierre de Gondy receives all,[1]

Ruggieri defiles all,

Mad Siblot reviles all,

The bilboquets please all,

The sarbacanes tease all,

The Duc de Guise tries all,

Rare Crichton outvies all,

Abbé Brantôme retails all,

Bussy d'Amboise assails all,

Old Ronsard recants all,

Young Jodelle enchants all,

Fat Villequier crams all,

His Holiness damns all,

Esclairmonde bright outshines all,

And wisely declines all,

La Rebours will bless all,

La Fosseuse confess all,

[1] Bishop of Paris.

La Guyol will fly all,

Torigni deny all,

John Calvin misguide all,

Wise Chicot deride all,

Spanish Philip[1] may crave all,

The Béarnais[2] brave all,

THE DEVIL WILL HAVE ALL!

[1] Philip II.
[2] Henri of Navarre, afterwards Henri IV.

DEATH TO THE HUGUENOT.

Death to the Huguenot! fagot and flame,

Death to the Huguenot! torture and shame!

Death! Death!

Heretics' lips sue for mercy in vain,

Drown their loud cries in the waters of Seine!

Drown! Drown!

Hew down, consume them with fire and with sword!

A good work ye do in the sight of the Lord!

Kill! Kill!

Hurl down their temples! their ministers slay!

Let them bleed as they bled on Barthélemy's day!

Slay! Slay!

LA GITANILLA.[1]

I.

By the Guadalquivir,
  Ere the sun be flown,
By that glorious river
  Sits a maid alone.
Like the sunset splendour
  Of that current bright,
Shone her dark eyes tender
  As its witching light;
Like the ripple flowing,
  Tinged with purple sheen,
Darkly, richly glowing,
  Is her warm cheek seen.
      'Tis the Gitanilla
        By the stream doth linger,
      In the hope that eve
        Will her lover bring her.

Set to music by Mr. F. Romer and Lady Stracey.

II.

See, the sun is sinking;

All grows dim, and dies;

See, the waves are drinking

Glories of the skies.

Day's last lustre playeth

On that current dark;

Yet no speck betrayeth

His long looked-for bark.

'Tis the hour of meeting!

Nay, the hour is past;

Swift the time is fleeting!

Fleeteth hope as fast?

Still the Gitanilla

By the stream doth linger,

In the hope that night

Will her lover bring her.

III.

Swift that stream flows on,

   Swift the night is wearing,—

Yet she is not gone,

   Though with heart despairing.

Dips an oar-plash—hark!—

   Gently on the river;

'Tis her lover's bark,

   On the Guadalquivir.

Hark! a song she hears!

   Every note she snatches.

As the singer nears,

   Her own name she catches.

     Now the Gitanilla

       Stays not by the water,

     For the midnight hour

       Hath her lover brought her.

THE TWICE-USED RING.[1]

"BEWARE thy bridal day!"

On her deathbed sighed my mother;

"Beware, beware, I say,

Death shall wed thee, and no other.

Cold the hand shall grasp thee,

Cold the arms shall clasp thee,

Colder lips thy kiss shall smother!

Beware thy bridal kiss!

"Thy wedding-ring shall be

From a clay-cold finger taken

From one that, like to thee,

Was by her love forsaken.

[1] Set to music by Mr. F. Romer.

For a twice-used ring

Is a fatal thing;

Her griefs who wore it are partaken—

    Beware that fatal ring!

" The altar and the grave

Many steps are not asunder;

Bright banners o'er thee wave,

Shrouded horror lieth under.

    Blithe may sound the bell,

    Yet 'twill toll thy knell;

Scathed thy chaplet by the thunder—

    Beware thy blighted wreath!"

Beware my bridal day!

Dying lips my doom have spoken;

Deep tones call me away;

From the grave is sent a token.

    Cold, cold fingers bring.

    That ill-omened ring;

Soon will a *second* heart be broken!

    This is my bridal day!

THE SOUL-BELL.[1]

Fast the sand of life is failing,
Fast her latest sigh exhaling,
    Fast, fast, is she dying.

With death's chills her limbs are shivering,
With death's gasp her lips are quivering,
    Fast her soul away is flying.

O'er the mountain-top it fleeteth,
And the skiey wonders greeteth,
Singing loud as stars it meeteth
    On its way.

[1] Set to music by Mr. F. Romer.

Hark! the sullen Soul-bell tolling,

Hollowly in echoes rolling,

Seems to say—

" She will ope her eyes—oh, never!

Quenched their dark light—gone for ever!

She is dead."

HYMN TO SAINT THECLA.[1]

In my trouble, in my anguish,
  In the depths of my despair,
As in grief and pain I languish,
  Unto thee I raise my prayer.
Sainted virgin! martyr'd maiden!
  Let thy countenance incline
Upon one with woes o'erladen,
  Kneeling lowly at thy shrine;
That in agony, in terror,
  In her blind perplexity,
Wandering weak in doubt and error,
  Calleth feebly upon thee.
Sinful thoughts, sweet saint, oppress me,
  Thoughts that will not be dismissed;
Temptations dark possess me,
  Which my strength may not resist.

[1] Set to music by Mr. F. Romer.

I am full of pain, and weary

  Of my life; I fain would die;

Unto me the world is dreary;

  To the grave for rest I fly.

For rest!—oh! could I borrow

  Thy bright wings, celestial Dove!

They should waft me from my sorrow,

  Where Peace dwells in bowers above.

    Upon one with woes o'erladen,

      Kneeling lowly at thy shrine;

    Sainted virgin! martyr'd maiden!

    Let thy countenance incline!

      Mei miserere Virgo,

      Requiem æternam dona!

By thy loveliness, thy purity,

  By thy spirit undefiled,

That in serene security

  Upon earth's temptations smiled;—

By the fetters that constrain'd thee,

  By thy flame-attested faith,

By the fervour that sustain'd thee,

    By thine angel-ushered death;—

By thy soul's divine elation,

    'Mid thine agonies assuring

Of thy sanctified translation

    To beatitude enduring;—

By the mystic interfusion

    Of thy spirit with the rays,

That in ever-bright profusion

    Round the Throne Eternal blaze:—

By thy portion now partaken,

    With the pain-perfected Just;

Look on one of hope forsaken,

    From the gates of mercy thrust.

      Upon one with woes o'erladen,

        Kneeling lowly at thy shrine,

      Sainted virgin! martyr'd maiden!

        Let thy countenance incline!

          Ora pro me mortis horâ!

          Sancta Virgo, oro te!

          Kyrie Eleison!

HYMN TO SAINT CYPRIAN.

HEAR! oh! hear me, sufferer holy,
  Who didst make thine habitation
'Mid these rocks, devoting wholly
  Life to one long expiation
Of thy guiltiness, and solely
  By severe mortification
Didst deliver thee. Oh! hear me!
  In my dying moments cheer me.
    By thy penance, self-denial,
    Aid me in the hour of trial.

May, through thee, my prayers prevailing
  On the Majesty of Heaven,
O'er the hosts of hell, assailing
  My soul, in this dark hour be driven!

So my spirit, when exhaling,

May of sinfulness be shriven,

And his gift unto the Giver

May be rendered pure as ever!

By thy own dark, dread possession.

Aid me with thine intercession!

THE CHURCHYARD YEW.

—————— Metuendaque succo
Taxus.

A noxious tree is the churchyard Yew,

As if from the dead its sap it drew;

Dark are its branches, and dismal to see,

Like plumes at Death's latest solemnity.

Spectral and jagged, and black as the wings

Which some spirit of ill o'er a sepulchre flings:

Oh! a terrible tree is the churchyard yew;

Like it is nothing so dreary to view.

Yet this baleful tree hath a core so sound,

Can nought so tough in the grove be found:

From it were fashioned brave English bows,

The boast of our isle, and the dread of its foes.

For our sturdy sires cut their stoutest staves

From the branch that hung o'er their father's graves;

And though it be dreary and dismal to view,

Stanch at the heart is the churchyard yew.

BLACK BESS.[1]

I.

Let the lover his mistress's beauty rehearse,

And laud her attractions in languishing verse;

Be it mine in rude strains, but with *truth* to express,

The love that I bear to my bonny Black Bess.

II.

From the West was her dam, from the East was her sire,

From the one came her swiftness, the other her fire;

No peer of the realm better blood can possess

Than flows in the veins of my bonny Black Bess.

III.

Look! look! how that eyeball glows bright as a brand!

That neck proudly arches, those nostrils expand!

Mark that wide-flowing mane! of which each silky tress

Might adorn prouder beauties—though none like Black Bess.

[1] Set to music by Mr. F. Romer.

IV.

Mark that skin sleek as velvet, and dusky as night,

With its jet undisfigured by one lock of white;

That throat branched with veins, prompt to charge or caress:

Now is she not beautiful?—bonny Black Bess!

V.

Over highway and by-way, in rough and smooth weather,

Some thousands of miles have we journeyed together;

Our couch the same straw, and our meal the same mess:

No couple more constant than I and Black Bess!

VI.

By moonlight, in darkness, by night, or by day,

Her headlong career there is nothing can stay;

She cares not for distance, she knows not distress:

Can you show me a courser to match with Black Bess?

VII.

Once it happened in Cheshire, near Dunham, I popped

On a horseman alone, whom I suddenly stopped;

That I lightened his pockets you'll readily guess—

Quick work makes Dick Turpin when mounted on Bess.

VIII.

Now it seems the man knew me; "Dick Turpin," said he,

" You shall swing for this job, as you live, d'ye see;"

I laughed at his threats and his vows of redress;

I was sure of an *alibi* then with Black Bess.

IX.

The road was a hollow, a sunken ravine,[1]

Overshadowed completely by wood like a screen;

I clambered the bank, and I needs must confess

That one touch of the spur grazed the side of Black Bess.

X.

Brake, brook, meadow, and ploughed field, Bess fleetly bestrode,

As the crow wings her flight we selected our road;

[1] The exact spot where Turpin committed this robbery, which has often been pointed out to me, lies in what is now a woody hollow, though once the old road from Altringham to Knutsford, skirting Dunham Park, and descending the hill that brings you to the bridge crossing the river Bollin. With some difficulty I penetrated this ravine. It is just the place for an adventure of the kind A small brook wells through it; and the steep banks are overhung with timber, and were, when I last visited the place, in April, 1834, a perfect nest of primroses and wild flowers. Hough (pronounced Hoo) Green lies about three miles across the country—the way Turpin rode. The old Bowling-green used to be one of the pleasantest inns in Cheshire.

We arrived at Hough Green in five minutes, or less—
My neck it was saved by the speed of Black Bess.

XI.

Stepping carelessly forward, I lounge on the green,
Taking excellent care that by all I am seen ;
Some remarks on time's flight to the squires I address,
But I say not a word of the flight of Black Bess.

XII.

I mention the hour—it was just about four—
Play a rubber at bowls—think the danger is o'er;
When athwart my next game, like a checkmate at chess,
Comes the horseman in search of the rider of Bess.

XIII.

What matter details?   Off with triumph I came;
He swears to the hour, and the squires swear the same;
I had robbed him at *four!*—while at four *they* profess
I was quietly bowling—all thanks to Black Bess!

XIV.

Then one halloo, boys, one loud cheering halloo!

To the swiftest of coursers, the gallant, the true!

For the sportsman unborn shall the memory bless

Of the horse of the highwayman—bonny Black Bess!

THE OLD OAK COFFIN.

Sic ego componi versus in ossa velim.—TIBULLUS.

In a churchyard, upon the sward, a coffin there was laid,

And leaning stood, beside the wood, a sexton on his spade.

A coffin old and black it was, and fashioned curiously,

With quaint device of carved oak, in hideous fantasie.

For here was wrought the sculptured thought of a tormented face,

With serpents lithe that round it writhe, in folded strict embrace.

Grim visages of grinning fiends were at each corner set,

And emblematic scrolls, mort-heads, and bones together met.

" Ah, well-a-day !" that sexton grey unto himself did cry,

" Beneath that lid much lieth hid—much awful mystery.

It is an ancient coffin from the abbey that stood here ;

Perchance it holds an abbot's bones, perchance those of a frere.

"In digging deep, where monks do sleep, beneath yon cloister

    shrined,

That coffin old, within the mould, it was my chance to find;

The costly carvings of the lid I scraped full carefully,

In hope to get at name or date, yet nothing could I see.

"With pick and spade I've plied my trade for sixty years and

    more,

Yet never found, beneath the ground, shell strange as that before;

Full many coffins have I seen—have seen them deep or flat,

Fantastical in fashion—none fantastical as that."

And saying so, with heavy blow, the lid he shattered wide,

And, pale with fright, a ghastly sight that sexton grey espied;

A miserable sight it was, that loathsome corpse to see,

The last, last, dreary, darksome stage of fall'n humanity.

Though all was gone, save reeky bone, a green and grisly heap,

With scarce a trace of fleshy face, strange posture did it keep.

The hands were clench'd, the teeth were wrench'd, as if the

    wretch had risen,

E'en after death had ta'en his breath, to strive and burst his prison.

The neck was bent, the nails were rent, no limb or joint was
    straight;
Together glued, with blood imbued, black and coagulate.
And, as the sexton stooped him down to lift the coffin plank,
His fingers were defiled all o'er with slimy substance dank.

" Ah, well-a-day!" that sexton grey unto himself did cry,
" Full well I see how Fate's decree foredoomed this wretch to
    die;
A living man, a breathing man, within the coffin thrust,
Alack! alack! the agony ere he returned to dust."

A vision drear did then appear unto that sexton's eyes;
Like that poor wight before him straight he in a coffin lies.
He lieth in a trance within that coffin close and fast;
Yet though he sleepeth now, he feels he shall awake at last.

The coffin then, by reverend men, is borne with footsteps slow,
Where tapers shine before the shrine, where breathes the requiem
    low;
And for the dead the prayer is said, for the soul that is *not* flown—
Then all is drown'd in hollow sound, the earth is o'er him thrown!

He draweth breath—he wakes from death to life more horrible;

To agony! such agony! no living tongue may tell.

Die! die he must, that wretched one! he struggles—strives in

    vain;

No more heaven's light, nor sunshine bright, shall he behold again.

"Gramercy, Lord!" the sexton roar'd, awakening suddenly,

"If this be dream, yet doth it seem most dreadful so to die.

Oh, cast my body in the sea! or hurl it on the shore!

But nail me not in coffin fast—no grave will I dig more."

Fantastical Ballads.

THE SORCERERS' SABBATH.[1]

I.

AROUND Montfaucon's mouldering stones,

The wizard crew is flitting;

And 'neath a Jew's unhallowed bones.

Man's enemy is sitting.

[1] Le Loyer observes, that the "Saboe-evohe," sung at the orgia, or Bacchanalia, agree with the exclamations of the conjurers and witches—"Her Sabat—Sabat!" and that Bacchus, who was only a devil in disguise, was named Sabassus, from the Sabbath of the Bacchanals. The accustomed form of their initiation was expressed in these words,—"I have drunk of the drum, and eaten of the cymbal; and am become a proficient;" which Le Loyer explains in the following manner:—By the cymbal is meant the caldron used by the modern conjurers to boil those infants they intend to eat; and by the drum, the goat's skin, blown up, whence they extract its moisture, boil it up fit to drink, and by that means are admitted to participate in the ceremonies of Bacchus. It is also alleged the name Sabbath is given to these assemblies of conjurers, because they are generally held on Saturdays.—*Monsieur Oufle. Description of the Sabbath.*

Terrible it is to see

Such fantastic revelry!

Terrible it is to hear

Sounds that shake the soul with fear!

Like the chariot wheels of Night,

  Swiftly round about they go;

Scarce the eye can track their flight,

  As the mazy measures flow.

Now they form a ring of fire;

Now a spiral, funeral pyre:—

Mounting now, and now descending,

In a circle never ending.

As the clouds the storm-blast scatters—

As the oak the thunder shatters—

As scared fowl in wintry weather—

They huddle, groan, and scream together.

Strains unearthly and forlorn

Issue from yon wrinkled horn;

By the bearded Demon blown,

Sitting on that great gray stone.

  Round with whistle and with whoop,

  Sweep the ever-whirling troop:

Streams of light their footsteps trail,

Forked as a comet's tail.

"Her Sabat!—Sabat!"—they cry—

An abbess joins their company.

II.

Sullenly resounds the roof,

With the tramp of horned hoof,—

Rings each iron-girdled rafter

With intolerable laughter:

Shaken by the stunning peal,

The chain-hung corses swing and reel.

From its perch on a dead-man's bone,

Wild with fright, hath the raven flown;

Fled from its feast hath the flesh-gorged rat:

Gone from its roost is the vampire bat;

Stareth and screameth the screech-owl old,

As he wheeleth his flight through the moonlit wold;

Bays the garbage-glutted hound,

Quakes the blind mole underground.

Hissing glides the speckled snake;

Loathliest things their meal forsake.

From their holes beneath the wall,

Newt, and toad, and adder crawl—

In the Sabbath-dance to sprawl!

Round with whistle and with whoop,

Sweep the ever-whirling troop;

Louder grows their frantic glee—

Wilder yet their revelry,

"Her Sabat!—Sabat!"—they cry,

A young girl joins their company.

III.

See that dark-hair'd girl advances—

In her hand a poignard glances;

On her bosom, white and bare,

Rests an infant passing fair:

Like a thing from heavenly region,

'Mid that diabolic legion.

Lovelier maid was never seen

Than that ruthless one, I ween:

Shape of symmetry hath she,

And a step as wild-doe free.

Her jetty hair is all unbound,

And its long locks sweep the ground.

Hushed in sleep her infant lies—

"Perish! child of sin," she cries,

"To fiends thy frame I immolate—

To fiends thy soul I dedicate!

Unbaptised, unwept, unknown—

In hell thy sire may claim his own."

From her dark eyes fury flashes—

From her breast her babe she dashes.

Gleams the knife—her brow is wrinkled—

With warm blood her hand is sprinkled!

Without a gasp—without a groan,

Her slumbering infant's soul hath flown.

At Sathan's feet the corse is laid—

To Sathan's view the knife display'd.[1]

A roar of laughter shakes the pile—

A mocking voice exclaims the while :—

[1] Sathan will have an ointment composed of the flesh of unbaptised children, that these innocents, being deprived of their lives by these wicked witches, their poor little souls may be deprived of the glories of Paradis *—De Lancre.*

"By this covenant—by this sign,

False wife! false mother! thou art mine!

Weal or wo, whate'er betide,

Thy doom is sealed, infanticide!

Shall nor sire's nor brother's wrath,

Nor husband's vengeance cross thy path;

And on him, thy blight, thy bane,

Hell's consuming fire shall reign!"

  Round with whistle and with whoop,

  Sweep the ever-whirling troop;

  In the caldron bubbling fast,

  The babe is by its mother cast!

  "Eman hetan!" shout the crew,

  And their frenzied dance renew.

IV.

The Fiend's wild strains are heard no more—

Dabbled in her infant's gore,

The new-made witch the caldron stirs—

Howl the demon-worshippers.

Now begin the Sabbath ——

Sathan marks his proselytes ;[1]

And each wrinkled hag anoints

With unguents rank her withered joints.

Unimaginable creeds—

Unimaginable deeds—

Foul, idolatrous, malicious,

Baleful, black, and superstitious,

Every holy form profaning,

Every sacred symbol staining,

Each foul sorcerer observes,

At the feet of him he serves.

——Here a goat is canonized,

Here a bloated toad baptised;

Bells around its neck are hung,

Velvet on its back is flung;

Mystic words are o'er it said,

Poison on its brow is shed.[2]

[1] The devil marks the sorcerers in a place which he renders insensible. And this mark is, in some, the figure of a hare; in others, of a toad's foot, or a black cat.—*Delrio, Disquisitiones Magicæ.*

[2] As the sabbath toads are baptised, and dressed in red or black velvet, with a bell at their neck, and another at each foot, the male sponsor holds the head, the female the feet.—*De Lancre.*

Here a cock of snowy plume,

Flutters o'er the caldron's fume;

By a Hebrew Moohel slain,

Muttering spells of power amain.[1]

——There within the ground is laid

An image that a foe may fade,

Priest unholy, chanting faintly

Masses weird with visage saintly;

While respond the howling choir

Antiphons from dark grimoire.[2]

Clouds from out the caldron rise,

Shrouding fast the star-lit skies.

[1] The sacrifice of a snow-white cock is offered by the Jews at the Feast of the Reconciliation. This was one of the charges brought against the Maréchale D'Ancre, condemned under Louis XIII. for sorcery and Judaism. Another absurd accusation, to which she pleaded guilty, was the eating of rams' kidneys! Those kidneys, however, we are bound to state, had been blessed as well as deviled. From Cornelius Agrippa we learn that the blood of a white cock is a proper suffumigation to the sun; and that, if pulled in pieces, while living, by two men, according to the ancient and approved practice of the Methonenses, the disjecta membra of the unfortunate bird will repel all unfavourable breezes. The reader of Rabelais, will also call to mind what is said respecting le cocq blanc in the chapter of Gargantua, treating "de ce qu'est signifié par les couleurs blanc et bleu!"

[2] "The Black Book."

Like ribs of mammoth through the gloom,

Hoar Montfaucon's pillars loom:

Wave its dead—a grisly row—

In the night-breeze to and fro.

At a beck from Sathan's hand,

Drop to earth that charnel band,—

Clattering as they touch the ground

With a harsh and jarring sound.

Their fluttering rags, by vulture rent,

A ghastly spectacle present ;

Flakes of flesh of livid hue,

With the white bones peeping through.

Blue phosphoric lights are seen

In the holes where eyes have been :

Shining through each hollow skull,

Like the gleam of lantern dull !

——Hark ! they shake their manacles—

Hark ! each hag responsive yells !

And her freely-yielded waist

Is by fleshless arms embraced,

Once again begins the dance—

How they foot it—how they prance !

Round the gibbet-cirque careering,

On their grinning partners fleering,

While, as first amid their ranks,

The new-made witch with Sathan pranks.

——Furious grows their revelry,—

But see!—within the eastern sky,

A bar of gold proclaims the sun—

Hark! the cock crows—all is done!

 With a whistle and a whoop,

 Vanish straight the wizard troop;

 On the bare and blasted ground,

 Horned hoofs no more resound:

 Caldron, goat, and broom are flown,

 And Montfaucon claims its own.

INCANTATION.

I.

Lovely spirit, who dost dwell

In the bowers invisible,

By undying Hermes reared,

By Stagyric sage revered,

Where the silver fountains wander,

Where the golden streams meander,

Where the dragon vigil keeps

Over mighty treasure heaps ;

Where the mystery is known,

Of the wonder working Stone;

Where the quintessence is gained,

And immortal life attained—

Spirit by this spell of power,

I call thee from thy viewless bower.

II.

The charm is wrought—the word is spoken

And the sealed vial broken!

Element with element

Is incorporate and blent;

Fire with water—air with earth,

As before creation's birth;

Matter gross is purified,

Matter humid rarefied;

Matter volatile is fixed,

The spirit with the clay commixed.

Laton is by azoth purged,

And the argent-vif disgorged;

And the black crow's head is ground,

And the magistery found;

And with broad empurpled wing

Springs to light the blood-red king,

By this fiery assation—

By this wondrous permutation

Spirit, from thy burning sphere

Float to earth—appear—appear!

THE WONDROUS STONE.

I.

Within the golden portal

Of the garden of the wise,

Watching by the seven-spray'd fountain,

The Hesperian Dragon lies.[1]

---

[1] These lines are little more than a versification of some of the celebrated President D'Espagnet's hermetic canons, with which the English adept must be familiar in the translation of Elias Ashmole. D'Espagnet's Arcanum Philosophiæ Hermeticæ has attained a classical celebrity among his disciples, at one period sufficiently numerous. The subjoined interpretation of this philosophical allegory may save the uninitiated reader some speculation. "La Fontaine que l'on trouve à l'entrée du Jardin est le Mercure des Sages, qui sort des sept sources, parce qu'il est le principe des sept métaux, et qu'il est formé par les sept planetes, quoique le soleil seul soit appelé son père et la lune seule sa mère. Le Dragon qu'on y fait boire est la putrefaction qui survient à la matière qui'ls ont appelée Dragon, à cause de sa couleur noire, et de sa puanteur. Ce Dragon quitte ses vêtemens, lorsque la couleur grise succède à la noire. Vous ne réussirez point si Vénus et Diane ne vous sont favorables, c'est-à-dire, si par le régime de feu, vous ne parvenez à

Like the ever-burning branches

In the dream of holy seer ;

Like the types of Asia's churches

Those glorious jets appear

Three times the magic waters

Must the Winged Dragon drain :

Then his scales shall burst asunder,

And his heart be reft in twain.

Forth shall flow an emanation,

Forth shall spring a shape divine,

And if Sol and Cynthia aid thee,

Shall the charmed Key be thine.

II.

In the solemn groves of Wisdom,

Where black pines their shadows fling

blanchir la matière qu'il appelle dans cet état de blancheur le règne de la lune."—*Dictionnaire Mytho-Hermetique.* The mysterious influence of the number Seven, and its relations with the planets, is too well known to need explanation here. Jacques Bohom has noticed it in the enigma contained in his *Aquarium Sapientium*, beginning—

Septem sunt urbes, septem pro more metalla,
Suntque dies septem, septimus est numerus.

κ. τ. λ.

Near the haunted cell of Hermes,

Three lovely flow'rets spring:

The violet damask-tinted,

In scent all flowers above;

The milk-white vestal lily,

And the purple flower of love.

Red Sol a sign shall give thee

Where the sapphire violets gleam,

Watered by the rills that wander

From the viewless golden stream,

One violet shalt thou gather—

But ah!—beware, beware!—

The lily and the amaranth

Demand thy chiefest care.[1]

[1] Vous ne séparerez point ces fleurs de leur racines—c'est-à-dire, qu'il ne faut rien ôter du vase. Par ce moyen on aura d'abord des violettes de couleur de saphir foncé, ensuite de lys, et enfin l'amaranthe, ou la couleur de pourpre, qui est l'indice de la perfection du souffre aurifique.—*Dict. Mytho-Herm.*

III.

Within the lake of crystal,[1]

Roseate as the sun's first ray,

With eyes of diamond lustre,[2]

A thousand fishes play.

A net within that water,

A net with web of gold;

If cast where air-bells glitter,

One shining fish shall hold.

IV.

Amid the oldest mountains,[3]

Whose tops are next the sun,

The everlasting rivers

Through glowing channels run.

[1] Les philosophes ont souvent donné le nom du Lac à leur vase, et au mercure, qui y est renfermé.—*Dict. Mytho-Herm.*

[2] Lorsque la matière est parvenue à un certain degré de cuisson, il se forme sur sa superficie de petites boules qui ressemblent aux yeux des poissons.—*Dict. Mytho-Herm.*

[3] Quelquefois les Alchemistes ont entendu par le terme de Montagne leur vase, leur fourneau, et toute matière métallique.—*Dict. Mytho-Herm.*

Those mountains are of silver,

    Those channels are of gold;

And thence the countless treasures

    Of the kings of earth are rolled;

But far—far must he wander

    O'er realms and seas unknown,

Who seeks the ancient mountains,

    Where shines the WONDROUS STONE!

THE CRYSTAL VASE.

In that mystic vase doth lie

Life and immortality.

Life to him who droops in death,

To the gasping bosom breath.

Immortality alone

To him to whom the " Word" is known.

Take it—'tis a precious boon

Vouchsafed by Hermes to his son.

THE NAMELESS WITCH.

On the smouldering fire is thrown

Tooth of fox and weasel bone,

Eye of cat, and skull of rat,

And the hooked wing of bat,

Mandrake root and murderer's gore,

Henbane, hemlock, hellebore,

Stibium, storax, bdellium, borax,

Ink of cuttle-fish and feather

Of the screech-owl, smoke together,

II.

On the ground is a circle traced;

On that circle a seal is placed;

On that seal is a symbol graven;

On that symbol an orb of heaven;

By that orb is a figure shown;
By that figure a name is known:
Wandering witch it is thine own!—

But thy name must not be named,
Nor to mortal ears proclaimed.

Shut are the leaves of the Grimoire dread;
The spell is muttered—the word is said,
And that word, in a whisper drowned,
Shall to thee like a whirlwind sound.

Swift through the shivering air it flies—
Swiftly it traverses earth and skies;
Wherever thou art—above—below—
Thither that terrible word shall go.

Art thou on the waste alone,
To the white moon making moan?
Art thou, human eye eschewing,
In some cavern philters brewing?

By familiar swart attended—

By a triple charm defended—

Gatherest thou the grass that waves

O'er dank pestilential graves ?—

Or on broom or goat astride,

To thy Sabbath dost thou ride ?

Or with sooty imp doth match thee ?

From his arms my spell shall snatch thee.

Shall it seek thee—and find thee,

And with a chain bind thee ;

And through the air whirl thee,

And at my feet hurl thee !

By the word thou dreadst to hear !

Nameless witch !—appear—appear !

THE TEMPTATION OF SAINT ANTHONY.[1]

SAINT ANTHONY weary

Of hermit-cell dreary,

Of penance, and praying,

Of orison saying,

Of mortification,

And fleshly vexation,

By good sprites forsaken,

By sin overtaken,

On flinty couch lying,

For death, like Job, crying,

[1] See Callot's magnificent piece of diablerie upon this subject, and the less extravagant, but not less admirable, picture of Teniers; and what will well bear comparison with either, Retzch's illustration of the Walpurgis Night Revels of Göethe.

THE TEMPTATION OF SAINT ANTHONY.

Was suddenly shrouded

By thick mists, that clouded

All objects with vapour,

And through them, like taper,

A single star shimmered,

And with blue flame glimmered.

II.

What spell then was muttered

May never be uttered;

Saint Anthony prayed not—

Saint Anthony stayed not—

But down—down descending

Through caverns unending,

Whose labyrinths travel

May never unravel,

By thundering torrent,

By toppling crag horrent,

All perils unheeding,

As levin swift speeding,

Habakkuk out-vying

On seraph-wing flying,

Was borne on fiend's pinion

To Hell's dark dominion.

III.

Oh! rare is the revelry

Of Tartarus' devilry!

Above him—around him—

On all sides surround him—

With wildest grimaces

Fantastical faces!

Here huge bats are twittering,

Strange winged mice flittering,

Great horned owls hooting,

Pale hissing stars shooting,

Red fire-drakes careering

With harpies are fleering.

Shapes whizzing and whirling,

Weird Sabbath-dance twirling,

Round bearded goat scowling,

Their wild refrain howling—

"Alegremonos Alegremos

Quegente nue va tenemos."[1]

IV.

Here Lemures, Lares,

Trolls, foliots, fairies,

Nymph, gnome, salamander,

In frolic groups wander.

Fearful shapes there are rising,

Of aspect surprising,

Phantasmata Stygia,

Spectra prodigia !

Of aspect horrific,

Of gesture terrific.

[1] According to Delancre, the usual refrain of the Sorcerers' Sabbath-song. See his "Description of the Inconstancy of Evil Angels and Demons." "Delancre's Description of the Witches' Sabbath," observes the amusing author of Monsieur Oufle, "is so very ample and particular, that I don't believe I should be better informed concerning it if I had been there myself."

Where caldrons are seething,

Lithe serpents are wreathing,

And wizards are gloating

On pois'nous scum floating,

While skull and bone placed out

In circle are traced out.

Here witches air-gliding

On broomsticks are riding,

A hag a faun chases,

A nun Pan embraces.

Here mimic fights waging,

Hell's warriors are raging;

Each legion commanding

A chief is seen standing.

Beelzebub gleaming,

Like Gentile god seeming—

Proud Belial advancing,

With awful ire glancing;

Asmodeus the cunning,

Abaddon, light shunning,

Dark Moloch deceiving,

His subtle webs weaving;

Meressin air-dwelling,

Red Mammon gold-telling.

v.

The Fiend, then dissembling,

Addressed the saint trembling:

"These are thine if down bowing,

Unto me thy soul vowing,

Thy worship thou'lt offer."

"Back, Tempter, thy proffer

With scorn is rejected."

"Unto me thou'rt subjected,

For thy doubts, by the Eternal!"

Laughed the Spirit Infernal.

At his word then compelling,

Forth rushed from her dwelling

A shape so inviting,

Enticing, delighting,

With lips of such witchery,

Tongue of such treachery,

(That sin-luring smile is

The torment of Lilis,)

Like Eve in her Eden,

Our father misleading.

With locks so wide flowing

Limbs so bright-glowing ;—

That Hell hath bewrayed him

If Heaven do not aid him.

" Her charms are surrendered

If worship is rendered."

" Sathan, get thee behind me

My sins no more blind me—

By Jesu's temptation !

By lost man's salvation !

Be this vision banished !"

And straight Hell evanished.

INSCRIPTION ON A GOLDEN KEY.

Gold! who wert a father's bane,

Gold! who wert a mother's stain,

Gold! be thou a daughter's chain

Of purity.

Shield her breast from sword and fire,

From intemperate desire;

From a heaven-abandon'd sire,

In charity!"

A MIDNIGHT MEETING OF THE LANCA-SHIRE WITCHES.

[SCENE—*The Ruined Conventual Church of Whalley Abbey.*]

MOTHER MOULD-HEELS.

Head of monkey, brain of cat,

Eye of weasel, tail of rat,

Juice of mugwort, mastic, myrrh—

All within the pot I stir.

OLD WIZARD.

Here is foam from a mad dog's lips,

Gather'd beneath the moon's eclipse,

Ashes of a shroud consumed,

And with deadly vapour fumed.

These within the mess I cast—

Stir the caldron—stir it fast!

A Red-haired Witch.

Here are snakes from out the river,

Bones of toad and sea-calf's liver;

Swine's flesh fatten'd on her brood,

Wolf's tooth, hare's foot, weasel's blood.

Skull of ape and fierce baboon,

And panther spotted like the moon;

Feathers of the horned owl,

Daw, pie, and other fatal fowl.

Fruit from fig-tree never sown,

Seed from cypress never grown.

All within the mess I cast,

Stir the caldron—stir it fast!

Malison.

In his likeness it is moulded,

In his vestments 'tis enfolded.

Ye may know it, as I show it!

In the breast sharp pins I stick,

And I drive them to the quick.

They are in—they are in—

And the wretch's pangs begin.

Now his heart

Feels the smart

Through his marrow,

Sharp as arrow,

Torments quiver

He shall shiver,

He shall burn,

He shall toss, and he shall turn,

Unavailingly.

Aches shall rack him

Cramps attack him;

He shall wail,

Strength shall fail,

Till he die

Miserably!

THIRD WITCH.

Over mountain, over valley, over woodland, over waste,

On our gallant broomsticks riding, we have come with frantic

  haste,

And the reason of our coming, as ye wot well, is to see

Who this night, as new-made witch. to our ranks shall added be.

SECOND WIZARD.

Beat the water, Demdike's daughter!

  Till the tempest gather o'er us:

Till the thunder strike with wonder

  And the lightnings flash before us!

Beat the water, Demdike's daughter!

Ruin seize our foes, and slaughtei !

ELIZABETH DEVICE.

Mount, water, to the skies!

Bid the sudden storm arise.

Bid the pitchy clouds advance,

Bid the forked lightnings glance,

Bid the angry thunder growl,

Bid the wild wind fiercely howl!

Bid the tempest come amain,

Thunder, lightning, wind, and rain!

CHORUS.

Beat the water, Demdike's daughter!

See the tempest gathers o'er us;

Lightning flashes—thunder crashes,

Wild winds sing in lusty chorus!

MOTHER CHATTOX.

Here is juice of poppy bruised,

With black hellebore infused;

Here is mandrake's bleeding root,

Mix'd with moonshade's deadly fruit:

Viper's bag, with venom fill'd,

Taken ere the beast was kill'd;

Adder's skin, and raven's feather,

With shell of beetle blent together;

Dragonwort and barbatus,

Hemlock black and poisonous;

Horn of hart, and storax red,

Lapwing's blood, at midnight shed.

In the heated pan they burn,

And to pungent vapours turn,

By this strong suffumigation,

By this potent invocation,

Spirits! I compel you here!

All who list my call appear!

INVOCATION.

White-robed brethren, who of old,

Nightly paced yon cloisters cold,

Sleeping now beneath the mould!

       I bid ye rise.

Abbots! by the weakling fear'd,

By the credulous revered,

Who this mighty fabric rear'd!

       I bid ye rise!

And thou last and guilty one![1]

By thy lust of power undone,

Whom in death thy fellows shun!

I bid thee come!

And thou, fair one,[2] who disdain'd

To keep the vows thy lips had feign'd;

And thy snowy garments stain'd!

I bid thee come!

MRS. NUTTER.

Thy aid I seek, infernal Power!

Be thy word sent to Malkin Tower,

That the beldame old may know

Where I will thou'dst have her go—

What I will, thou'dst have her do!

EVIL SPIRIT.

Thou who seek'st the Demon's aid,

Know'st the price that must be paid.

[1] John Paslew, last Abbot of Whalley. Capitale affectus supplicio—1537.

[2] Isole de Heton

MRS. NUTTER.

Spirit, grant the aid I crave,

And that thou wishest thou shalt have.

Another worshipper is won,

Thine to be when all is done.

EVIL SPIRIT.

Enough, proud witch, I am content.

To Malkin Tower the word is sent,

Forth to her task the beldame goes,

And where she points the streamlet flows;

Its customary bed forsaking,

Another distant channel making.

Round about like elfets tripping,

Stock and stone, and tree are skipping;

Halting where she plants her staff,

With a wild exulting laugh.

   Ho! ho! 'tis a merry sight,

   Thou hast given the hag to-night.

Lo! the sheepfold, and the herd,

To another site are stirr'd!

And the rugged limestone quarry,

Where 'twas digg'd may no more tarry;

While the gobiin-haunted dingle,

With another dell must mingle.

Pendle Moor is in commotion,

Like the billows of the ocean,

When the winds are o'er it ranging,

Heaving, falling, bursting, changing,

    Ho! ho! 'tis a merry sight,

    Thou hast given the hag to night.

Lo! the moss-pool sudden flies,

In another spot to rise;

And the scanty-grown plantation

Finds another situation,

And a more congenial soil,

Without needing woodman's toil.

Now the warren moves—and see!

How the burrowing rabbits flee,

Hither, thither till they find it,

With another brake behind it.

    Ho! ho! 'tis a merry sight,

    Thou hast given the hag to-night.

Lo! new lines the witch is tracing,

Every well-known mark effacing,

Elsewhere, other bounds erecting,

So the old there's no detecting.

    Ho! ho! 'tis a pastime quite,

    Thou hast given the hag to-night.

The hind at eve, who wander'd o'er

The dreary waste of Pendle Moor,

Shall wake at dawn, and in surprise,

Doubt the strange sight that meets his e

The pathway leading to his hut

Winds differently—the gate is shut.

The ruin on the right that stood,

Lies on the left, and nigh the wood;

The paddock fenced with wall of stone,

Well-stock'd with kine, a mile hath flown,

The sheepfold and the herd are gone.

Through channels new the brooklet rushes,

Its ancient course conceal'd by bushes.

Where the hollow was a mound

Rises from the upheaved ground.

Doubting, shouting with surprise,

How the fool stares, and rubs his eyes!

All so changed, the simple elf

Fancies he is changed himself!

    Ho! ho! 'tis a merry sight

    The hag shall have when dawns the light.

    But see! she halts and waves her hand,

    All is done as thou hast plann'd.

THE MANDRAKE.[1]

Μῶλύ δέ μιν καλέουσι θεοί, χαλεπὸν δέ τ' ὀρύσσειν
'Ανδράσι γε θνητοῖσι, θεοὶ δέ τε πάντα δύνανται.

HOMERUS.

THE mandrake grows 'neath the gallows-tree,

And rank and green are its leaves to see;

Green and rank, as the grass that waves

Over the unctuous earth of graves;

---

[1] The supposed malignant influence of the mandrake is frequently alluded to by our elder dramatists; and with one of the greatest of them, Webster (as might be expected from a muse revelling like a ghoul in graves and sepulchres), the plant is an especial favourite. But none have plunged so deeply into the subject as Sir Thomas Browne. He tears up the fable root and branch. Concerning the danger ensuing from eradication of the mandrake, he thus writes:—" The last assertion is, that there follows a hazard of life to them that pull it up, that some evil fate pursues them, and that they live not very long hereafter. Therefore the attempt hereof among the ancients was not in ordinary way; but, as Pliny informeth, when they intended to take up the root of this plant, they took the wind thereof, and

And though all around it be bleak and bare,

Freely the mandrake flourisheth there.

Maranatha—Anathema !

Dread is the curse of mandragora !

Euthanasy !

At the foot of the gibbet the mandrake springs,

Just where the creaking carcase swings ;

Some have thought it engendered

From the fat that drops from the bones of the dead ;

Some have thought it a human thing ;

But this is a vain imagining,

Maranatha—Anathema !

Dread is the curse of mandragora !

Euthanasy !

with a sword describing three circles about it, they digged it up, looking toward the west. A conceit not only injurious unto truth and confutable by daily experience, but somewhat derogatory unto the providence of God ; that is, not only to impose so destructive a quality on any plant, but to conceive a vegetable whose parts are so useful unto many, should, in the only taking up, prove mortal unto any. This were to introduce a second forbidden fruit, and enhance the first malediction, making it not only mortal for Adam to taste the one, but capital for his posterity to eradicate, or dig up the other."—*Vulgar Errors,* book ii. c. **vi.**

A charnel leaf doth the mandrake wear,

A charnel fruit doth the mandrake bear;

Yet none like the mandrake hath such great power,

Such virtue resides not in plant or flower;

Aconite, hemlock, or moonshade, I ween,

None hath a poison so subtle and keen.

> *Maranatha—Anathema !*
>
> *Dread is the curse of mandragora !*
>
> *Euthanasy !*

And whether the mandrake be create

Flesh with the flower incorporate,

I know not; yet, if from the earth 'tis rent,

Shrieks and groans from the root are sent;

Shrieks and groans, and a sweat like gore,

Oozes and drops from the clammy core.

> *Maranatha—Anathema !*
>
> *Dread is the curse of mandragora !*
>
> *Euthanasy !*

Whoso gathereth the mandrake shall surely die;

Blood for blood is his destiny.

Some who have plucked it have died with groans,

Like to the mandrake's expiring moans;

Some have died raving, and some beside,

With penitent prayers—but *all* have died.

 Jesu! save us by night and by day!

  From the terrible death of mandragora!

   Euthanasy!

EPHIALTES..

I.

I RIDE alone—I ride by night

Through the moonless air on a courser white !

Over the dreaming earth I fly,

Here and there—at my phantasy !

My frame is withered, my visage old,

My locks are frore, and my bones ice-cold.

The wolf will howl as I pass his lair,

The ban-dog moan, and the screech-owl stare.

For breath, at my coming, the sleeper strains,

And the freezing current forsakes his veins !

Vainly for pity the wretch may sue—

Merciless Mara no prayers subdue !

> *To his couch I flit—*
>
> *On his breast I sit—*
>
> *Astride ! astride ! astride !*
>
> *And one charm alone*
>
> *(A hollow stone !* [1]*)*
>
> *Can scare me from his side !*

II.

A thousand antic shapes I take ;

The stoutest heart at my touch will quake.

The miser dreams of a bag of gold,

Or a ponderous chest on his bosom rolled.

[1] In reference to this imaginary charm, Sir Thomas Browne observes, in his *Vulgar Errors,* "What natural effects can reasonably be expected, when, to prevent the Ephialtes, or Nightmare, we hang a hollow stone in our stables?"   Grose also states, "that a stone with a hole in it, hung at the bed's head, will prevent the nightmare, and is therefore called a hag-stone."   The belief in this charm still lingers in some districts, and maintains, like the horse-shoe affixed to the barn-door, a feeble stand against the superstition-destroying "march of intellect."

The drunkard groans 'neath a cask of wine;

The reveller swelts 'neath a weighty chine.

The recreant turns, by his foes assailed,

To flee!—but his feet to the ground are nailed.

The goatherd dreams of the mountain-tops,

And, dizzily reeling, downward drops.

The murderer feels at his throat a knife,

And gasps, as his victim gasp'd for life!

The thief recoils from the scorching brand;

The mariner drowns in sight of land!

—Thus sinful man have I power to fray,

Torture and rack—but not to slay!

But ever the couch of purity,

With shuddering glance I hurry by.

> *Then mount! away!*
>
> *To horse! I say,*
>
> *To horse! astride! astride!*
>
> *The fire-drake shoots—*
>
> *The screech-owl hoots—*
>
> *As through the air I glide!*

THE CORPSE-CANDLE.

Lambere flamma ταφος et circum funera pasci.

I.

THROUGH the midnight gloom did a pale blue light
To the churchyard mirk wing its lonesome flight :—
Thrice it floated those old walls round—
Thrice it paused—till the grave it found.
Over the grass-green sod it glanced,
Over the fresh-turned earth it danced,
Like a torch in the night-breeze quivering—
Never was seen so gay a thing !
Never was seen so blithe a sight
As the midnight dance of that pale blue light !

II.

Now what of that pale blue flame dost know ?
Canst tell where it comes from, or where it will go ?

Is it the soul, released from clay,

Over the earth that takes its way,

And tarries a moment in mirth and glee

Where the corse it hath quitted interr'd shall be?

Or *is* it the trick of some fanciful sprite,

That taketh in mortal mischance delight,

And marketh the road the coffin shall go,

And the spot where the dead shall be soon laid low?

Ask him who can answer these questions aright;

I know not the cause of that pale blue light!

THE HAND OF GLORY.[1]

FROM the corse that hangs on the roadside tree

(A murderer's corse it needs must be),

Sever the right hand carefully :—

Sever the hand that the deed hath done,

Ere the flesh that clings to the bones be gone ;

In its dry veins must blood be none.

Those ghastly fingers white and cold,

Within a winding-sheet enfold ;

Count the mystic count of seven :

Name the Governors of heaven.[2]

Then in earthen vessel place them,

And with dragon-wort encase them,

---

[1] See the celebrated recipe for the Hand of Glory in "Les Secrets d
Petit Albert."

[2] The seven planets, so called by Mercurius Trismegistus.

Bleach them in the noonday sun,

Till the marrow melt and run,

Till the flesh is pale and wan,

As a moon-ensilvered cloud,

As an unpolluted shroud.

Next within their chill embrace

The dead man's awful candle place;

Of murderer's fat must that candle be

(You may scoop it beneath the roadside tree),

Of wax, and of Lapland sisame.

Its wick must be twisted of hair of the dead,

By the crow and her brood on the wild waste shed.

Wherever that terrible light shall burn

Vainly the sleeper may toss and turn;

His leaden lids shall he ne'er unclose

So long as the magical taper glows.

Life and treasure shall he command

Who knoweth the charm of the Glorious Hand!

But of black cat's gall let him aye have care,

And of screech-owl's venomous blood beware!

THE CARRION CROW.[1]

I.

THE Carrion Crow is a sexton bold,

He raketh the dead from out of the mould;

He delveth the ground like a miser old,

Stealthily hiding his store of gold. *Caw! Caw!*

The Carrion Crow hath a coat of black,

Silky and sleek like a priest's to his back;

Like a lawyer he grubbeth—no matter what way—

The fouler the offal, the richer his prey.

Caw! Caw! the Carrion Crow!

Dig! Dig! in the ground below!

[1] Set to music by Mr. F. Romer.

II.

The Carrion Crow hath a dainty maw,

With savory pickings he crammeth his craw;

Kept meat from the gibbet it pleaseth his whim,

It never can *hang* too long for him!   *Caw! Caw!*

The Carrion Crow smelleth powder, 'tis said,

Like a soldier escheweth the taste of cold lead;

No jester, or mime, hath more marvellous wit,

For, wherever he lighteth, he maketh a hit!

Caw! Caw! the Carrion Crow!
Dig! Dig! in the ground below!

THE HEADSMAN'S AXE.

I.

THE axe was sharp, and heavy as lead,

As it touched the neck, off went the head!

Whir—whir—whir—whir !

II.

Queen Anne[1] laid her white throat upon the block,

Quietly waiting the fatal shock;

The axe it severed it right in twain,

And so quick—so true—that she felt no pain!

Whir—whir—whir—whir

III.

Salisbury's Countess, she would not die

As a proud dame should—decorously.

[1] Anne Boleyn.

Lifting my axe, I split her skull,

And the edge for a month it was notched and dull.

Whir—whir—whir—whir !

IV.

Queen Catherine Howard gave me a fee,—

A chain of gold—to die easily :

And her costly present she did not rue,

For I touched her head and away it flew !

Whir—whir—whir—whir !

Humorous Ballads

Humorous Ballads

THE CHRONICLE OF GARGANTUA:

SHOWING HOW HE TOOK AWAY THE GREAT BELLS OF NOTRE-DAME.

I.

GRANDGOUSIER was a toper boon, as Rabelais will tell ye,

Who, once upon a time, got drunk with his old wife Gargamelly:

Right royally the bout began (no queen was more punctilious

Than Gargamelle) on chitterlings, botargos, godebillios ![1]

Sing, Carimari, carimara! golynoly, golynolo!

II.

They licked their lips, they cut their quips—a flask then each

selected;

And with good Greek, as satin sleek, their gullets they humected.

---

[1] " Gaudebillaux sont grasses trippes de coiraux. Coiraux sont bœufs engresses à la criche, et prés guimaulx. Prés guimaulx sont qui portent herbe deux foys l'an."—RABELAIS.

Rang stave and jest, the flask they pressed—but ere away the
  wine went,
Occurred most unexpectedly Queen Gargamelle's confinement !
        Sing, Carimari, carimara ! golynoly, golynolo !

III.

No sooner was GARGANTUA born, than from his infant throttle
Arose a most melodious cry to his nurse to bring the bottle !
Whereat Grandgousier much rejoiced—as it seemed, unto his
  thinking,
A certain sign of a humour fine for most immoderate drinking !
        Sing, Carimari, carimara ! golynoly, golynolo !

IV.

Gargantua shot up, like a tower some city looking over !
His full-moon visage in the clouds, leagues off, ye might
  discover !
His gracious person he arrayed—I do not mean to laugh at ye—
With a suit of clothes, and great trunk hose, of a thousand ells
  of taffety.
        Sing, Carimari, carimara ! golynoly, golynolo !

V.

Around his waist Gargantua braced a belt of silk bespangled,

And from his hat, as a platter flat, a long blue feather dangled ;

And down his hip, like the mast of ship, a rapier huge

    descended,

With a dagger keen, stuck his sash between, all for ornament

    intended.

        Sing, Carimari, carimara ! golynoly, golynolo !

VI.

So learned did Gargantua grow, that he talked like one whose

    turn is

For logic, with a sophister, hight Tubal Holofernes.

In Latin, too, he lessons took from a tutor old and seedy,

Who taught the " Quid est," and the " Pars,"—one Jobelin de

    Bridé !

        Sing, Carimari, carimara ! golynoly, golynolo !

VII.

A monstrous mare Gargantua rode—a black Numidian courser—

A beast so droll, of filly or foal, was never seen before sir !

Great elephants looked small as ants, by her side—her hoofs were

    cloven!

Her tail was like the spire at Langes—her mane like goat-beards

    woven!

        Sing, Carimari, carimara! golynoly, golynolo!

VIII.

Upon this mare Gargantua rode until he came to Paris,

Which, from Utopia's capital, as we all know, rather far is—

The thundering bells of Notre Dame he took from out the steeple,

And he hung them round his great mare's neck in the sight of

    all the people!

        Sing, Carimari, carimara! golynoly, golynolo!

IX.

Now, what Gargantua did beside, I shall pass by without notice,

As well as the absurd harangue of that wiseacre Janotus;

But the legend tells that the thundering bells Bragmardo brought

    away, sir,

And that in the towers of Notre-Dame they are swinging to this

    day, sir!

        Sing, Carimari, carimara! golynoly, golynolo!

X.

Now the great deeds of Gargantua,—how his father's foes he
    followed—

How pilgrims six, with their staves and scrips, in a lettuce-leaf
    he swallowed—

How he got blind drunk with a worthy monk, Friar Johnny of
    the Funnels,—

And made huge cheer, till the wine and beer flew about his camp
    in runnels—

      Sing, Carimari, carimara! golynoly, golynolo!

XI.

How he took to wife, to cheer his life, fat Badebec the moper;

And by her begat a lusty brat, Pantagruel the toper!

And did other things, as the story sings, too long to find a place
    here,

Are they not writ, with matchless wit, by Alcofribas Nasier ?[1]

      Sing, Carimari, carimara! golynoly, golynolo!

---

[1] The anagram of François Rabelais

MY OLD COMPLAINT:

ITS CAUSE AND CURE.

I'M sadly afraid of my Old Complaint—

Dying of thirst.—Not a drop I've drunk

For more than an hour : 'Tis too long to wait.

Wonderful how my spirits have sunk!

Provocation enough it is for a saint,

To suffer so much from my Old Complaint !

II.

What is it like, my Old Complaint ?

I'll tell you anon, since you wish to know.

It troubles me now, but it troubled me first,

When I was a youngster, years ago !

MY OLD COMPLAINT.

"I'm sadly afraid of my old complaint."

Bubble-and-squeak is the image quaint;—

Of what it is like, my Old Complaint!

III.

The Herring, in a very few minutes, we're told,

  Loses his life, ta'en out o' the sea;

Rob me of Wine, and you will behold

  Just the same thing happen to me.

    Thirst makes the poor little Herring so faint;—

    THIRST is the Cause of my Old Complaint!

IV.

The bibulous Salmon is ill content,

  Unless he batheth his jowl in brine:

And so, my spirits are quickly spent,

  Unless I dip *my* muzzle in Wine!

    Myself in the jolly old Salmon I paint:—

    WINE is the Cure of my Old Complaint.

      Give me full bottles and no restraint,

      And little you'll hear of my Old Complaint!

V.

I never indulge in fanciful stuff,

  Or idly prate, if my flagon be full;

Give me good Claret, and give me enough,

  And then my spirits are never dull.

  Give me good Claret and no constraint;

  And I soon get rid of my Old Complaint!

        Herring and Salmon my friends will acquaint

        With the Cause and the Cure of my Old Complaint

JOLLY NOSE.[1]

I.

JOLLY nose! the bright rubies that garnish thy tip

Are dug from the mines of canary;

And to keep up their lustre I moisten my lip

With hogsheads of claret and sherry.

II.

Jolly nose! he who sees thee across a broad glass

Beholds thee in all thy perfection;

And to the pale snout of a temperate ass

Entertains the profoundest objection.

[1] Arranged by Mr. G. Herbert Rodwell.

III.

For a big-bellied glass is the palette I use,

    And the choicest of wine is my colour;

And I find that my nose takes the mellowest hues

    'The fuller I fill it—the fuller!

IV.

Jolly nose! there are fools who say drink hurts the sight;

    Such dullards know nothing about it;

'Tis better, with wine, to extinguish the light,

    Than live always in darkness, without it.

THE

WINE DRINKER'S DECLARATION.

TO ALL AND SUNDRY WHOM IT MAY CONCERN.

I.

The Toper who knows how to empty his can,

Is not half so afraid of a highwayman,

As he is of indifferent tipple:

With the last a stout fellow may fight for his purse;

Of the other the consequence certain is worse,

Down the throat if permitted to ripple.

II.

If acetose claret I happen to sip,

'Tis my wish, as the beaker I dash from my lip,

That my throat to a short span would dwindle;

But when I get hold of the vintage I prize,

I care not, although it should shoot out in size,

Until like a crane's neck it spindle.

III.

All wat'ry potations I let 'em alone,

And never will use such, until I am grown

   A Hermit, and dwell in a cavern ;

But then the good Anchorite brandy must get

(An anker, right often,) his whistle to wet,

   Or else he will sigh for the tavern.

IV.

My maxim is ever to drink of the best,

And in that I resemble sound soakers at rest ;

   Our Fathers we always should follow :

Old customs, old manners, we never should quit,

Or the world will judge us, as some folks judge of it,

   And declare our professions are hollow.

WITH MY BACK TO THE FIRE.

I.

WITH my back to the fire, and my paunch to the table

Let me eat,—let me drink as long as I am able;

Let me eat,—let me drink whate'er I set my whims on,

Until my nose is blue, and my jolly visage crimson.

II.

The doctor preaches abstinence, and threatens me with dropsy,

But such advice, I needn't say, from drinking never stops ye :—

The man who likes good liquor is of nature brisk and brave,
boys,

So drink away !—drink while you may !—there's no drinking in
the grave, boys.

THE OLD WATER-DRINKER'S GRAVE.

I.

A STINGY curmudgeon lies under the stone,
Who ne'er had the heart to get mellow;—
A base water-drinker!—I'm glad he is gone,
We're well rid of the frowsy old fellow.

II.

You see how the nettles environ his grave!
Weeds only could spring from his body.
While his heirs spend the money he fasted to save,
In wine and in women—the noddy!

CIDER OF DEVONSHIRE.

I.

CIDER good of Devonshire—

That just now is my desire.

Let the blockheads laugh, who will,

Quick, mine host, the flagon fill

With the admirable juice,

Which the apple-vats produce.

Better 'tis, I will maintain,

Than the stuff you call champagne.

Thirst I feel—and my desire

Is the drink of Devonshire.

II.

Cider fine ! thou hast the merit,

With thy lightness and thy spirit,

Not to mystify the brain!

You may fill, and fill again.

Quaff as much as you require

Of the drink of Devonshire.

III.

'Tis the property of cider—

Ne'er to make a breach the wider.

With your friend you would not quarrel

Were you to consume a barrel.

Idle bickering and fooling

Dwell not in this liquor cooling.

Generous thoughts alone inspire

Draughts of dulcet Devonshire.

IV.

Cider sparkling, cider placid,

False it is to call it acid.

To the light you hold the cup,

How the atoms bright leap up!

How the liquid foams and bubbles,

Ready to dispel your troubles!

How its fragrancy invites!

How its flavour fine delights,

As the lip and throat it bites!

Pour it down! you'll never tire

Of delicious Devonshire!

VENITE POTEMUS.[1]

I.

VENITE, jovial sons of Hesper,

Who from matin unto vesper,

    Roam abroad sub Domino ;

Benedictine, Carmelite,

Quaff we many a flask to-night

    Salutari nostro.

If the wine be, as I think,

Fit for reverend lips to drink

    Jubilemus ei.

Ecce bonum vinum, venite potemus !

II.

Hodie, when cups are full,

Not a thought or care should dull

    Corda vestra.

[1] Adapted from an old French Imitatoyre Bachique.

ALE AND SACK.

I.

Your Gaul may tipple his thin, thin wine,

And prate of its hue, and its fragrance fine,

Shall never a drop pass throat of mine

      Again—again !

His claret is meagre (but let that pass),

I can't say much for his hippocrass,

And never more will I fill my glass

      With cold champagne.

II.

But froth me a flagon of English ale,

Stout, and old, and as amber pale,

Which heart and head will alike assail—

      Ale—ale be mine !

Or brew me a pottle of sturdy sack,

Sherris and spice, with a toast to its back,

And need shall be none to bid me attack

                That drink divine !

D R U I D.

I.

Through the world have I wandered wide,

With never a wife, or a friend by my side,

Save Druid—a comrade staunch and tried :—

Troll on away !

Druid, my dog, is a friend in need,

Druid, my dog, is a friend indeed,

Druid, my dog, is of English breed!

More need I say ?

—Troll on away !

II.

Druid would perish my life to save,

For faithful Druid like fate I'd brave,

The dog and his master shall find one grave,

Troll on away !

Life! I heed not its loss a feather!

And when black Atropos snaps my tether,

She must cut twice—we'll die together!

                    No more I'll say.

                    —Troll on away!

THE THIRTY REQUISITES.[1]

Thirty points of perfection each judge understands,

The standard of feminine beauty demand

Three white :—and, without further prelude, we know

That the skin, hands, and teeth, should be pearly as snow.

Three black :—and our standard departure forbids

From dark eyes, darksome tresses, and darkly-fringed lids.

Three red :—and the lover of comeliness seeks

For the hue of the rose in the lips, nails, and cheeks.

Three long :—and of this you, no doubt, are aware ?

Long the body should be, long the hands, long the hair.

[1] Imitated from a *trentaine* of *beaux Sis*, recorded in the *Dames Galantes*. Brantôme gives them in Spanish prose from the lips of a fair Toledan; they are, however, to be met with in an old French work anterior to our chronicler, entitled *De la Louange et Beauté des Dames*. The same maxims have been turned into Latin hexameters by François Corniger (an ominous name for a writer on such a subject), and into Italian verse by Vincentio Calmeta.

Three short :—and herein nicest beauty appears—

Feet short as a fairy's, short teeth, and short ears.

Three large :—and remember this rule as to size,

Embraces the shoulders, the forehead, the eyes.

Three narrow :—a maxim to every man's taste—

Circumference small in mouth, ankle, and waist.

Three round :—and in this I see infinite charms—

Rounded fulness apparent in leg, hip, and arms.

Three fine :—and can aught the enchantment eclipse,

Of fine tapering fingers, fine hair, and fine lips ?

Three small :—and my thirty essentials are told—

Small head, nose, and bosom, compact in its mould.

Now the dame who comprises attractions like these,

Will require not the cestus of Venus to please ;

While he who has met with an union so rare,

Has had better luck than has fall'n to *my* share.

LOVE'S HOMILY.

Saint Augustin, one day, in a fair maiden's presence,

Declared that pure love of the soul is the essence!

And that faith be it ever so firm and potential,

If love be not its base, must prove uninfluential.

Saint Bernard, likewise, has a homily left us—

(Sole remnant of those, of which fate hath bereft us!)

Where the good Saint confers, without any restriction.

On those who love most, his entire benediction.

Saint Ambrose, again, in his treatise, "*De Virgine,*"

To love one another is constantly urging ye;

And a chapter he adds, where he curses—not blesses—

The ill-fated wight who no mistress possesses!

Wise De Lyra, hereon, makes this just observation,

That the way to the heart is the way to salvation;

And the further from love—we're the nearer damnation!

Besides, as remarks this profound theologian,

(Who was perfectly versed in the doctrine Ambrogian)—

He, who loves not, is worse than the infamous set ye call

Profane, unbelieving, schismatic, heretical;

For, if he the fire of one region should smother,

He is sure to be scorched by the flames of the other!

And this is the reason, perhaps, why Saint Gregory

(The Pope, who reduced the stout Arians to beggary)

Averred—(keep this counsel for ever before ye)

That the lover on earth has his sole purgatory!

Peroration.

Let your minds then be wrapp'd in devout contemplation

Of the precepts convey'd by this grave exhortation;

Be loving, beloved, and never leave off—it's

The way to fulfil both the law and the prophets!

A CHAPTER OF HIGHWAYMEN.

AIR—*" Which nobody can deny !"*

OF every rascal of every kind,

The most notorious to my mind,

Was the Cavalier Captain, gay JEMMY HIND ![1]

Which nobody can deny.

But the pleasantest coxcomb among them all

For lute, coranto, and madrigal,

Was the galliard Frenchman, CLAUDE DU-VAL ![2]

Which nobody can deny.

[1] James Hind (the "Prince of Prigs"), a royalist captain of some distinction, was hanged, drawn, and quartered, in 1652. Some good stories are told of him. He had the credit of robbing Cromwell, Bradshaw, and Peters. His discourse to Peters is particularly edifying.

[2] See Du-Val's life by Doctor Pope, or Leigh Hunt's brilliant sketch of him in *The Indicator.*

And Tobygloak never a coach could rob,

Could lighten a pocket or empty a fob,

With a neater hand than OLD MOB, OLD MOB![1]

Which nobody can deny.

Nor did housebreaker ever deal harder knocks

On the stubborn lid of a good strong box,

Than the prince of good fellows, TOM COX, TOM COX![2]

Which nobody can deny.

And blither fellow on broad highway,

Did never with oath bid traveller stay,

Than devil-may-care WILL HOLLOWAY![3]

Which nobody can deny.

[1] We cannot say much in favour of this worthy, whose name was Thomas Simpson. The reason of his *sobriquet* does not appear. He was not particularly scrupulous as to his mode of appropriation. One of his sayings is, however, on record. He told a widow whom he robbed, "that the end of a woman's husband begins in tears, but the end of her tears is another husband." "Upon which," says his chronicler, "the gentlewoman gave him about fifty guineas."

[2] Tom was a sprightly fellow, and carried his sprightliness to the gallows; for just before he was turned off he kicked Mr. Smith, the ordinary, and the hangman out of the cart—a piece of pleasantry which created, as may be supposed, no small sensation.

[3] Many agreeable stories are related of Holloway. His career, however,

And in roguery nought could exceed the tricks

Of GETTINGS and GREY, and the five or six,

Who trod in the steps of bold NEDDY WICKS![1]

Which nobody can deny.

Nor could any so handily break a lock

As SHEPPARD, who stood on the Newgate dock,

And nicknamed the jailers around him, "*his flock!*"[2]

Which nobody can deny.

closed with a murder. He contrived to break out of Newgate, but returned to witness the trial of one of his associates; when, upon the attempt of a turnkey, one Richard Spurling, to seize him, Will knocked him on the head in the presence of the whole court. For this offence he suffered the extreme penalty of the law in 1712.

[1] Wick's adventures with Madame Toly are highly diverting. It was this hero, not Turpin, as has been erroneously stated, who stopped the celebrated Lord Mohun. Of Gettings and Grey, and "the five or six," the less said the better.

[2] One of Sheppard's recorded *mots*. When a Bible was pressed upon his acceptance by Mr. Wagstaff, the chaplain, Jack refused it, saying, that in his situation one file would be worth all the Bibles in the world." A gentleman who visited Newgate asked him to dinner; Sheppard replied, "that he would take an early opportunity of waiting upon him." And we believe he kept his word.

Nor did highwayman ever before possess,

For ease, for security, danger, distress,

Such a mare as DICK TURPIN's Black Bess! Black Bess!

Which nobody can deny.

THE RAPPAREES.

Air—"*The Groves of the Pool.*"

Let the Englishman boast of his Turpins and Sheppards, as
    cocks of the walk,

His Mulsacks, and Cheneys, and Swiftnecks[1]—it's all botheration
    and talk ;

Compared with the robbers of Ireland, they don't come within
    half a mile,

There never were yet any rascals, like those of my own native isle.

First and foremost comes Redmond O'Hanlon, allowed the
    first thief of the world,[2]

That o'er the broad province of Ulster, the Rapparee banner
    unfurled ;

---

[1] A trio of famous High-Tobygloaks. Swiftneck was a captain of *Irish*
dragoons, by the bye.

[2] Redmond O'Hanlon was the Rob Roy of Ireland, and his adventures, many of which are exceedingly curious, would furnish as rich

Och! he was an elegant fellow, as ever you saw in your life,

At fingering the blunderbuss trigger, or handling the throat-

    cutting knife.

materials for the novelist, as they have already done for the ballad-mongers: some of them are, however, sufficiently well narrated in a pleasant little tome, published at Belfast, entitled *The History of the Rapparees*. We are also in possession of a funeral discourse preached at the obsequies of the "noble and renowned" Henry St. John, Esquire,, who was unfortunately killed by the *Tories* (the *Destructives* of those days), in the induction to which we find some allusion to Redmond. After describing the thriving condition of the north of Ireland, about 1680, the Rev. Lawrence Power, the author of the sermon, says, "One mischief there was, which, indeed, in a great measure destroyed all, and that was, a pack of insolent bloody outlaws, whom they here call *Tories*. These had so riveted themselves in these parts, that by the interest they had among the natives, and some English, too, *to their shame be it spoken*, they exercise a kind of separate sovereignty in three or four counties in the north of Ireland. REDMOND O'HANLON is their chief, and has been these many years; a cunning, dangerous fellow, who, though proclaimed an outlaw with the rest of his crew, and sums of money set upon their heads, yet he reigns still, and keeps all in subjection, so far that 'tis credibly reported *he raises more in a year by contribution à-la-mode de France than the king's land taxes and chimney-money come to, and thereby is enabled to bribe clerks and officers, IF NOT THEIR MASTERS, (!) and makes all too much truckle to him*." Agitation, it seems, was not confined to our own days—but the "finest country in the world" has been, and ever will be the same. The old game is played under a new colour—the only difference being, that had Redmond lived in our time, he would, in all probability, not only have pillaged a county, but *represented* it in parliament. The spirit of the Rapparee is still abroad—though we fear there is little of the *Tory*

And then such a dare-devil squadron as that which composed

   Redmond's *tail !*

Meel, Mactigh, Jack Reilly, Shan Bernagh, Phil Galloge, and

   Arthur O'Neal;

Shure never were any boys like 'em, for rows, agitation, and sprees;

Not a *rap* did they leave in the country, and hence they were

   called *Rap*parees.[1]

Next comes Power, the Great Tory[2] of Munster, a gentleman

   born every inch,

And strong Jack Macpherson of Leinster, a horse-shoe who

   broke at a pinch;

The last was a fellow so lively, not death e'en his courage could

   damp,

For as he was led to the gallows, he played his own "march to

   the camp."[3]

left about it. We recommend this note to the serious consideration of
the declaimers against the sufferings of the " six millions." (1834.)

[1] Here Titus was slightly in error. He mistook the cause for the effect.
"They were styled Rapparees," Mr. Malone says, "from being armed with
a half-pike, called by the Irish a *rapparee*."—Todd's Johnson.

[2] *Tory*, so called from the Irish word *Toree*, give me your money.—
Todd's Johnson.

[3] As he was carried to the gallows, Jack played a fine tune of his own

PADDY FLEMING, DICK BALF, and MULHONI, I think are the
next on my list,

All adepts in the beautiful science of giving a pocket a twist;

JEMMY CARRICK must follow his leaders, ould PURNEY who put
in a huff,

By dancing a hornpipe at Tyburn, and bothering the hangman
for snuff.

There's PAUL LIDDY, the curly-pate Tory, whose noddle was
stuck on a spike,

And BILLY DELANY, the "*Songster*,"[1] we never shall meet with
his like;

composing, on the bagpipe, which retains the name of Macpherson's tune
to this day.—*History of the Rapparees.*

[1] "Notwithstanding he was so great a rogue, Delany was a handsome
portly man, extremely diverting in company, and could behave himself
before gentlemen very agreeably. *He had a political genius* (not
altogether surprising in so eminent a *Tory*), and would have made a great
proficiency in learning if he had rightly applied his time. He composed
several songs, and put tunes to them; and by his skill in music gained the
favour of some of the leading musicians in the country, who endeavoured
to get him reprieved."—*History of the Rapparees.* The particulars of
the *Songster's* execution are singular:—"When he was brought into
court to receive sentence of death, the judge told him that he was informed

For his neck by a witch was anointed, and warranted safe by her
    charm,
No hemp that was ever yet twisted his wonderful throttle could
    harm.

And lastly, there's CAHIR NA CAPPUL, the handiest rogue of
    them all,
Who only need whisper a word, and your horse will trot out of
    his stall;

he should say 'that there was not a rope in Ireland sufficient to hang him.'
'But,' says he, 'I'll try if Kilkenny can't afford one strong enough to do
your business; and if that will not do, you shall have another and
another.' Then he ordered the sheriff to choose a rope, and Delany was
ordered for execution the next day. The sheriff having notice of his
mother boasting that no rope could hang her son (and pursuant to the
judge's desire), provided two ropes, but Delany broke them one after
the other! The sheriff was then in a rage, and went for three bed cords,
which he plaited three-fold together, *and they did his business!* Yet the
sheriff was afraid he was not dead; and in a passion, to make trial
stabbed him with his sword in the soles of his feet, and at last cut the
rope. After he was cut down, his body was carried into the court-house,
where it remained in the coffin for two days, standing up, till the judge
and all the spectators were fully satisfied he was stiff and dead, and
then permission was given to his friends to remove the corpse and bury
it."—*History of the Rapparees.*

Your tit is not safe in your stable, though you or your groom
should be near,

And devil a bit in the paddock, if CAHIR gets *hould* of his ear.

Then success to the Tories of Ireland, the generous, the gallant,
the gay !

With them the best *Rumpads*[1] of England are not to be named
the same day !

And were further proof wanting to show what precedence we
take with our *prigs,*

Recollect that *our* robbers are TORIES, while those of *your*
country are WHIGS !

[1] Highwaymen, as contradistinguished from footpads

A ROMANY CHANT.

A ROMANY CHANT.[1]

In a box[2] of the Stone Jug[3] I was born,

Of a hempen widow[4] the kid forlorn,

Fake away.

And my father, as I've heard say,

Fake away.

Was a merchant of capers[5] gay,

Who cut his last fling with great applause,

[6]Nix my doll pals, fake away.

Who cut his last fling with great applause,[7]

To the tune of a " hearty choke with caper sauce."

Fake away.

---

[1] Set to music by Mr. Rodwell. [2] Cell. [3] Newgate

[4] A woman whose husband has been hanged. [5] A dancing-master.

[6] " Nothing, comrades; on, on," supposed to be addressed by a thief to his confederates.

[7] Thus Victor Hugo, in " Le Dernier Jour d'un Condamné," makes an imprisoned felon sing :—

"Je le ferai danser une danse

Où il n'y a pas de plancher."

The knucks in quod[1] did my schoolmen play,

          Fake away.

And put me up to the time of day;

Until at last there was none so knowing,

          Nix my doll pals, fake away.

Until at last there was none so knowing,

No such sneaksman[2] or buzgloak[3] going.

          Fake away.

Fogles[4] and fawnies[5] soon went their way,

          Fake away.

To the spout[6] with the sneezers[7] in grand array.

No dummy hunter[8] had forks[9] so fly;

          Nix my doll pals, fake away.

No dummy hunter had forks so fly.

No knuckler[10] so deftly could fake a cly,[11]

          Fake away.

Thieves in prison.   [2] Shoplifter.   [3] Pickpocket.
[4] Handkerchiefs.   [5] Rings.   [6] To the pawnbroker.
[7] Snuff-boxes.   [8] Pickpocket.
[9] The two fore-fingers used in picking a pocket.
[10] Pickpocket.   [11] Pick a pocket.

No slour'd hoxter[1] my snipes[2] could stay,

>*Fake away.*

None knap a reader[3] like me in the lay.

Soon then I mounted in swell-street high.

>*Nix my doll pals, fake away.*

Soon then I mounted in swell-street high,

And sported my flashest toggery.[4]

>*Fake away,*

Firmly resolved I would make my hay,

>*Fake away.*

While Mercury's star shed a single ray;

And ne'er was there seen such a dashing prig,[5]

>*Nix my doll pals, fake away.*

And ne'er was there seen such a dashing prig,

With my strummel faked in the newest twig.[6]

>*Fake away.*

[1] No inside coat-pocket, buttoned up.

[2] Scissors.   [3] Steal a pocket-book.

[4] Best made clothes.   [5] Thief.

[6] With my hair dressed in the first fashion.

With my fawnied famms,[1] and my onions gay,[2]

> *Fake away ;*

My thimble of ridge,[3] and my driz kemesa ;[4]

All my togs were so niblike[5] and splash,

> *Nix my doll palls, fake away.*

All my togs were so niblike and splash,

Readily the queer screens I then could smash ;[6]

> *Fake away,*

But my nuttiest lady one fine day,

> *Fake away,*

To the beaks[7] did her fancy man betray,

And thus was I bowled out at last.[8]

> *Nix my doll pals, fake away.*

And thus was I bowled out at last,

And into the jug for a lag was cast ;[9]

> *Fake away.*

---

[1] With several rings on my hands.   [2] Seals.

[3] Gold watch.   [4] Laced shirt.

[5] Gentlemanlike.   [6] Easily then forged notes could I pass.

[7] Police.   [8] Taken at length.

[9] Cast for Transportation.

But I slipped my darbies[1] one morn in May,

Fake away.

And gave to the dubsman[2] a holiday.

And here I am, pals, merry and free,

A regular rollicking romany.[3]

Nix my doll pals, fake away.

[1] Fetters. [2] Turnkey. [3] Gipsy.

OLIVER WHIDDLES!

I.

Oliver whiddles—the tattler old !

Telling what best had been left untold.

Oliver ne'er was a friend of mine ;

All glims I hate that so brightly shine.

Give me a night black as hell, and then

See what I'll show to you, my merry men.

II.

Oliver whiddles !—who cares—who cares,

If down upon us he peers and stares ?

Mind him who will, with his great white face.

Boldly *I'll* ride by his glim to the chase ;

Give him a Rowlard, as loudly as ever

Shout, as I show myself, " Stand and deliver !"

WILL DAVIES AND DICK TURPIN.

WILL DAVIES AND DICK TURPIN.

Hodiè mihi, cràs tibi.—SAINT AUGUSTIN.

I.

ONE night when mounted on my mare,

To Bagshot Heath I did repair,

And saw Will Davis hanging there,

Upon the gibbet bleak and bare,

With a rustified, fustified, mustified air !

II.

Within his chains bold Will looked blue,

Gone were his sword and snappers too,

Which served their master well and true ;

Says I, "Will Davies, how are you ?

With your rustified, fustified, mustified air !"

III.

Says he, "Dick Turpin, here I be,

Upon the gibbet as you see;

I take the matter easily;

You'll have your turn as well as me,

　With your whistle-me, pistol-me, cut-my-throat air !"

IV.

Says I, "That's very true, my lad;

Meantime, with pistol and with prad,

I'm quite contented as I am,

And heed the gibbet not a d——n !

　　With its rustified, fustified, mustified air !"

V.

For never more shall Bagshot see

A highwayman of such degree,

Appearance, and gentility,

As Will, who hangs upon the tree.

　　With his rustified, fustified, mustified air !

THE FOUR CAUTIONS.

I.

Pay attention to these cautions four,

And through life you will need little more,

Should you dole out your days to threescore :—

Beware of a pistol before!

> Before! before!

Beware of a pistol before!

II.

And when backwards his ears are inclined,

And his tail with his ham is combined,

Caution two you will bear in your mind :—

Beware of a prancer behind!

> Behind! behind!

Beware of a prancer behind!

III.

Thirdly, when in the park you may ride,

On your best bit of blood, sir, astride.

Chatting gay to your old friend's young bride :—

Beware of a coach at the side!

> At the side! at the side!

Beware of a coach at the side!

IV.

Lastly, whether in purple or grey,

Canter, ranter, grave, solemn, or gay,

Whate'er he may do or may say :—

Beware of a priest every way!

> Every way! every way!

Beware of a priest every way!

THE DOUBLE CROSS.

BY A MEMBER OF THE P. C.

I.

THOUGH all of us have heard of *crost* fights,

And certain *gains*, by certain *lost* fights;

I rather fancies that it's news,

How in a mill, *both* men should *lose;*

For vere the *odds* are thus made *even*,

It plays the dickens with the *steven*;[1]

Besides, against all rule they're sinning,

Vere *neither* has *no* chance of vinning.

Ri, tol, lol, &c.

II.

Two *milling coves*, each vide avake,

Vere backed to fight for heavy stake;

----

[1] Money.

But in the mean time, so it vos,

Both *kids* agreed to *play a cross;*

Bold came each *buffer*[1] to the *scratch,*

To make it look a *tightish match;*

They *peeled*[2] in style, and bets were making,

'Tvos six to four, but few were *taking.*

Ri, tol, lol, &c.

III.

Quite cautiously the mill began,

For neither knew the other's plan;

Each *cull*[3] completely in the *dark,*

Of vot might be his neighbour's *mark;*

Resolved his *fibbing*[4] not to mind,

Nor yet to *pay him back in kind;*

So on each other *kept they tout,*[5]

And *spurred* a bit, and *dodged* about.

Ri, tol, lol, &c.

---

[1] Man.   [2] Stripped.   [3] Fellow.

[4] A particular kind of pugilistic punishment.

[5] Kept each an eye upon the other.

IV.

Vith *mawleys*[1] raised, Tom bent his back,

As if to plant a heavy thwack :

Vile Jem, vith neat left-handed *stopper*,

Straight threatened Tommy with a *topper*.

'Tis all my eye ! no claret flows,

No *facers* sound—no smashing blows.

Five minutes pass, yet not a *hit*,

How can it end, pals ?—Vait a bit.

Ri, tol, lol, &c.

V.

Each cove vos *teazed* with double duty,

To please his backers, yet *play booty ;*[2]

Ven, luckily for Jem, a *teller*

Vos planted right upon his *smeller ;*

Down dropped he, stunned ; ven time was called,

Seconds in vain the *seconds* bawled ;

The *mill* is o'er, the crosser *crost,*

The loser's *von,* the vinner's *lost !*

Ri, tol, lol, &c.

---

[1] Hands.　　　　　　　　[2] Deceive them.

THE MODERN GREEK.

(NOT TRANSLATED FROM THE ROMAIC.)

Come, gemmen, name, and make your game,
See, round the ball is spinning.
Black, red, or blue, the colours view,
Un, *deux*, *cinque*, 'tis beginning.
Then make your game,
The colour name,
While round the ball is spinning.

This sleight of hand my *flat* shall *land*,
While *covered* by my *bonnet*,[1]
I *plant* my ball, and boldly call,
Come make your game upon it!
Thus rat-a-tat!
I land my flat!
'Tis black—not red—is winning.

[1] Accomplice.

At gay *roulette* was never met

  A lance like mine for *bleeding!*

I'm ne'er *at fault*, at nothing halt,

  All other *legs* preceding.

    To all awake,

    I never shake

    A *mag*[1] unless I nip it.

Blind-hookey sees how well I squeeze

  The *well-packed* cards in shuffling.

Ecarté, whist, I never missed,

  And nick the *broads*[2] while ruffling.

    Mogul or loo,

    The same I do,

    I'm down to trumps as trippet!

French hazard ta'en, *I nick the main*,

  Was ne'er so prime a *caster*.

No *crabs* for me, I'm fly, d'ye see;

  The bank shall change its master.

[1] A farthing.   [2] Cards.

Seven *quatre, trois,*

The stakes are high!

Ten *mains!* ten *mains* are mine, pals!

At *Rouge et Noir,* yon *hellite*[1] choir

I'll make no bones of stripping;

One glorious *coup* for me shall *do,*

While they may deal each *pip* in.

Trente-un-après

Ne'er clogs my way;

The game—the game's divine, pals.

At billiards set I make my bet,

I'll *score* and win the *rub,* pals;

I miss my *cue,* my *hazard,* too,

But yet my foe I'll drub, pals.

That *cannon-twist,*

I ne'er had missed,

Unless to suit my views, pals.

To make all right, the match look *tight,*

This trick, you know, is done, pals;

[1] Gr. *élite.*—PRINTER'S DEVIL.

But now be gay, I'll *show* my play—

  Hurrah! the game is won, pals,

    No hand so fine,

    No wrist like mine,

  No odds I e'er refuse, pals.

Then choose your game; whate'er you name,

  To me alike all offers;

Chick-hazard, whist, whate'er you list,

  Replenish quick your coffers.

    Thus, rat-a-tat!

    I *land* my *flat!*

  To every purse I *speak*, pals.

Cramped boxes 'ware, all's right and fair,

  Barred balls I *bar* when goaded;

The deuce an ace is out of place!

  The deuce a die is *loaded!*

    Then make your game,

    Your colour name:

  Success attend the *Greek*, pals.

PLEDGE OF THE HIGHWAYMAN.

I.

Come, fill up a bumper to Eve's fairest daughters,

    Who have lavished their smiles on the brave and the free;

Toast the sweethearts of Dudley, Hind, Wilmot, and Waters,[1]

    Whate'er their attraction, whate'er their degree.

II.

Pledge! pledge in a bumper, each kind-hearted maiden,

    Whose bright eyes were dimmed at the highwayman's fall;

Who stood by the gallows with sorrow o'erladen,

    Bemoaning the fate of the gallant Du-Val!

[1] Four celebrated highwaymen, all rejoicing in the honourable distinction of captain.

III.

Here's to each lovely lass chance of war may bring near one,

    Whom, with courtier-like manner, politely we stop;

And to whom, like the lover addressing his dear one,

    In terms of entreaty *the question* we pop.

IV.

How oft, in such case, rosy lips have proved sweeter

    Than the rosiest book;—bright eyes saved a bright ring;

While that *one other* kiss has brought off a *repeater*,

    And a bead as a *favour*—the *favourite* string.

V.

With our hearts ready rifled, each pocket we rifle,

    With the pure flame of chivalry stirring our breasts ;

Life's risk for our mistress's praise is a trifle ;

    And each purse as a trophy our homage attests.

VI.

Then toss off your glasses to all girls of spirit,

    Ne'er with names, or with number, your memories vex :

Our toast, boys, embraces each woman of merit,

    And, for fear of omission, we'll drink the WHOLE SEX !

THE GAME OF HIGH TOBY.

I.

Now Oliver[1] puts his black nightcap on,

And every star its glim[2] is hiding,

And forth to the heath is the scampsman[3] gone,

His matchless cherry-black[4] prancer riding;

Merrily over the common he flies,

Fast and free as the rush of rocket,

His crape-covered vizard drawn over his eyes,

His tol[5] by his side, and his pops[6] in his pocket.

CHORUS.

Then who can name

So merry a game,

As the game of all games—high toby?[7]

---

[1] The moon.   [2] Light.   [3] Highwayman.

[4] "Cherry-coloured—black; there being black cherries as well as red."—GROSE.

[5] Sword.   [6] Pistols.   [7] Highway-robbery.

II.

The traveller hears him, away! away!

    Over the wide wide heath he scurries;

He heeds not the thunderbolt summons to stay,

    But ever the faster and faster he hurries.

But what daisy-cutter can match that black-tit?

    He is caught—he must " stand and deliver;"

Then out with the dummy,[1] and off with the bit,[2]

    Oh! the game of high toby for ever!

CHORUS.

*   Then who can name*

*   So merry a game,*

*   As the game of all games—high toby!*

III.

Believe me there is not a game, my brave boys,

    To compare with the game of high toby;

No rapture can equal the tobyman's joys,

    To blue devils, blue plumbs[3] give the go-by!

---

[1] Pocket-book.   [2] Money.   [3] Bullets.

And what if, at length, boys, he come to the crap![1]

Even rack punch has *some* bitter in it,

For the mare-with-three-legs,[2] boys, I care not a rap,

'Twill be over in less than a minute!

GRAND CHORUS.

Then hip, hurrah!

Fling care away!

Hurrah for the game of high toby!

[1] The gallows.   [2] Ditto.

THE SCAMPSMAN.

Quis verè rex?—SENECA.

THERE is not a king, should you search the world round,

So blithe as the king of the road to be found;

His pistol's his sceptre, his saddle his throne,

Whence he levies supplies, or enforces a loan.

Derry down.

To this monarch the highway presents a wide field,

Where each passing subject a tribute must yield;

His palace (the tavern!) receives him at night,

Where sweet lips and sound liquor crown all with delight,

Derry down.

The soldier and sailor, both robbers by trade,

Full soon on the shelf, if disabled, are laid:

The one gets a patch, and the other a peg,

But, while luck lasts, the highwayman shakes a loose leg !

Derry down.

Most fowls rise at dawn, but the owl wakes at e'en,

And a jollier bird can there nowhere be seen ;

Like the owl, our snug scampsman his snooze takes by day,

And, when night draws her curtain, scuds after his prey !

Derry down.

As the highwayman's life is the fullest of zest,

So the highwayman's death is the briefest and best ;

He dies not as other men die, by *degrees !*

But AT ONCE ! without wincing, and quite at his ease !

Derry down.

THE KNIGHT OF MALTA:

A CANTERBURY TALE.[1]

COME list to me, and you shall have, without a hem or haw, sirs,

A Canterbury pilgrimage, much better than old Chaucer's,

'Tis of a hoax I once played off, upon that city clever,

The memory of which, I hope, will stick to it for ever.

> *With my coal black beard, and purple cloak,*
>
> *jack-boots, and broad-brimmed castor,*
>
> *Iley-ho! for the knight of Malta!*

[1] This ballad describes pretty accurately the career of an extraordinary individual, who, in the lucid intervals of a half-crazed understanding, palmed himself off upon the good folk of Canterbury, in the year 1832, as a certain "SIR WILLIAM PERCY HONEYWOOD COURTENAY, KNIGHT OF MALTA;" and contrived—for there was considerable "method in his madness"—to support the deception during a long period. Imposture and credulity are of all ages; and the Courtenays of

To execute my purpose, in the first place you must know, sirs,

My locks I let hang down my neck—my beard and whiskers

grow, sirs;

A purple cloak I next clapped on, a sword tagged to my side,

sirs,

And mounted on a charger black, I to the town did ride, sirs.

With my coal-black beard, &c.

our own time are rivalled by the Tofts and Andrés of the last century.

The following account of the *soi-disant* SIR WILLIAM COURTENAY is extracted from "An Essay on his Character, and Reflections on his Trial," published at the theatre of his exploits:—"About Michaelmas last it was rumoured that an extraordinary man was staying at the Rose Inn of this city (Canterbury), who passed under the name of Count Rothschild, but had been recently known in London by the name of Thompson! This would have been sufficient to excite attention, had not other incidents materially added to the excitement. His costume and countenance denoted foreign extraction, while his language and conversation showed that he was well acquainted with almost every part of this kingdom. He was said to live with singular frugality, notwithstanding abundant samples of wealth, and professions of an almost unlimited command of money. He appeared to study retirement, if not concealment, although subsequent events have proved that society of every grade, beneath the middle class, is the element in which he most freely breathes. He often decked his person with a fine suit of Italian clothing, and sometimes with the more gay and imposing costume of the Eastern nations, yet these foreign habits were for months scarcely visible beyond the limits of the inn of his abode

Two pages were there by my side, upon two little ponies,

Decked out in scarlet uniform as spruce as macaronies;

Caparisoned my charger was, as grandly as his master,

And o'er my long and curly locks I wore a broad-brimmed

    castor.

With my coal-black beard, &c.

and the chapel not far from it, in which he was accustomed to offer his Sabbath devotions.   This place was the first to which he made a public and frequent resort; and though he did not always attempt to advance towards the uppermost seat in the synagogue, he attracted attention from the mere singularity of his appearance.

"Such was the eccentric, incongruous individual who surprised our city by proposing himself as a third candidate for its representation, and who created an entertaining contest for the honour, long after the sitting candidates had composed themselves to the delightful vision of an unexpensive and unopposed return.   The notion of representing the city originated beyond all doubt in the fertile brain of the man himself.   It would seem to have been almost as sudden a thought in his mind, as it was a sudden and surprising movement in the view of the city; nor have we been able to ascertain whether his sojourn at the Rose was the cause or the effect of his offering to advocate our interests in parliament— whether he came to the city with that high-minded purpose, or subsequently formed the notion, when he saw, or thought he saw, an opening for a stranger of enterprise like himself.

*   *   *   *   *

"As the county election drew on, we believe between the nomination on Barham Downs and the voting in the cattle market of the city, the draught of a certain handbill was sent to a printer of this city, with a

The people all flocked forth, amazed to see a man so hairy,

Oh! such a sight had ne'er before been seen in Canterbury!

My flowing robe, my flowing beard, my horse with flowing mane,

    sirs!

They stared—the days of chivalry they thought were come

    again, sirs!

                With my coal-black beard, &c.

request that he would publish it without delay. Our readers will not be surprised that he instantly declined the task; but as we have obtained possession of the copy, and its publication can now do no injury to any one, we entertain them with a sight of this delectable sample of Courtenay prudence and politeness.

"'O yes! O yes! O yes! I, Lord Viscount William Courtenay, of Powderham Castle, Devon, do hereby proclaim Sir Thomas Tylden, Sir Brook Brydges, Sir Edward Knatchbull, and Sir William Cosway, for cowards, unfit to represent, or to assist in returning members of parliament to serve the brave men of Kent.

"'Percy Honeywood Courtenay, of Hales and Evington Place, Kent, and Knight of Malta.

"'Any gentleman desiring to know the reasons why Lord Courtenay so publicly exposes backbiters, any man of honour shall have satisfaction at his hands, and in a public way, according to the laws of our land—trial by combat; when the Almighty God, the Lord of Hosts is his name, can decide the 'truth,' whether it is a libel or not. I worship truth as my God, and will die for it—and upon this we will see who is strongest, God or man.'

"It is a coincidence too curious to be overlooked, that this doughty

I told them a long rigmarole romance, that did not halt a

Jot, that they beheld in me a real knight of Malta!

Tom à Becket had I sworn I was, that saint and martyr

hallowed,

I doubt not just as readily the bait they would have swallowed.

With my coal-black beard, &c.

champion of *truth* should so soon have removed himself from public life by an act of deliberate and wanton perjury. We never read any of his rhapsodies, periodical or occasional, till the publication of this essay imposed the self-denying task upon us; but now we find that they abound in strong and solemn appeals to the *truth;* in bold proclamations that *truth* is his palladium; in evidences that he writes and raves, that he draws his sword and clenches his fist, that he expends his property and the property of others committed to his hands, in no cause but that of *truth !* His famous periodical contains much vehement declamation in defence of certain doctrines of religion, which he terms the truth of the sublime system of Christianity, and for which alone he is content to live, and also willing to die. All who deviate from his standard of truth, whether theological or moral, philosophical or political, he appears to consider as neither fit for life or death. Now it is a little strange, his warmest followers being witnesses, that such an advocate of truth should have become the willing victim of falsehood, the ready and eager martyr of the worst form of falsehood—perjury.

"The decline of his influence between the city and county elections has been partly attributed, and not without reason, to the sudden change in his appearance from comparative youth to advancing, if not extreme age. On the hustings of the city he shone forth in all the dazzling lustre of an

I rode about, and speechified, and everybody gullied,

The tavern-keepers diddled, and the magistracy bullied:

Like puppets were the townsfolk led in that show they call a

    raree;

The Gotham sages were a joke to those of Canterbury.

With my coal-black beard, &c.

Oriental chief; and such was the effect of gay clothing on the meridian of life, that his admirers, especially of the weaker sex, would insist upon it that he had not passed the beautiful spring-time of May. There were, indeed, some suspicious appearances of a near approach to forty, if not two or three years beyond it; but these were fondly ascribed to his foreign travels in distant and insalubrious climes; he had acquired his duskiness of complexion, and his strength of feature and violence of gesture, and his profusion of beard in Egypt and Syria, in exploring the catacombs of the one country, and bowing at the shrines of the other. On the other hand, the brilliancy of his eye, the melody of his voice, and the elasticity of his muscles and limbs, were sufficient arguments in favour of his having scarcely passed the limit that separates manhood from youth.

"All doubts on these points were removed, when the crowd of his fair admirers visited him at the retirement of his inn, in the intervals of his polling. These *sub Rosâ* interviews—we allude to the name of the inn, and not to anything like privacy there, which the very place and number of the visitors altogether precluded—convinced them that he was even a younger and livelier man than his rather boisterous behaviour in the hall would allow them to hope. In fact, he was now installed by acclamation *Knight of Canterbury as well as Malta, and King of Kent, as well as Jerusalem*

The theatre I next engaged, where I addressed the crowd, sirs,

And on retrenchment and reform, I spouted long and loud, sirs;

On tithes, and on taxation, I enlarged with skill and zeal, sirs,

Who so able as a Malta knight, the malt-tax to repeal, sirs?

With my coal-black beard, &c.

As a candidate I then stepped forth to represent their city,

And my non-election to that place was certainly a pity;

For surely I the fittest was, and very proper, very,

To represent the wisdom and the wit of Canterbury.

With my coal-black beard, &c.

At the trial of some smugglers next, one thing I rather queer
did,

And the justices upon the bench I literally *bearded;*

It became dangerous then to whisper a syllable of suspicion against his wealth or rank, his wisdom or beauty; and all who would not bow down before this golden image were deemed worthy of no better fate than Shadrach, Meschech, and Abednego—to be cast into a burning fiery furnace."

———————

As a sequel to the foregoing story, it may be added, that the Knight of Malta became the inmate of a lunatic asylum; and on his liberation was shot at the head of a band of Kentish hinds, whom he had deluded into the belief that he was the Messiah!

For I swore that I some casks did see, though proved as clear as
 day, sirs,
That I happened at the time to be some fifty miles away, sirs!

With my coal-black beard, &c.

The last assertion, I must own, was somewhat of a blunder,
And for perjury indicted they compelled me to knock under;
To my prosperous career this slight error put a stop, sirs,
And thus *crossed*, the knight of Malta was at length obliged to
 hop, sirs!

With his coal-black beard, and purple cloak,
jack-boots, and broad-brimmed castor.

Good-bye to the knight of Malta!

SAINT GILES'S BOWL.[1]

I.

WHERE Saint Giles's church stands, once a lazar-house stood;

And, chained to its gates, was a vessel of wood;

A broad-bottomed bowl, from which all the fine fellows,

Who passed by that spot on their way to the gallows,

Might tipple strong beer

Their spirits to cheer,

And drown in a sea of good liquor all fear!

For nothing the transit to Tyburn beguiles,

So well as a draught from the Bowl of Saint Giles!

[1] At the hospital of St. Giles for Lazars, the prisoners conveyed from the City of London towards Tyburn, there to be executed for treasons, felonies, or other trespasses, were presented with a Bowl of Ale, thereof to drink, as their last refreshing in this life.—*Strype's Stow.* Book ix. ch. iii.

II.

By many a highwayman many a draught

Of nutty-brown ale at Saint Giles's was quaft,

Until the old lazar-house chanced to fall down,

And the broad-bottom'd bowl was removed to the Crown,

> *Where the robber may cheer*
>
> *His spirits with beer,*
>
> *And drown in a sea of good liquor all fear!*
>
> *For nothing the transit to Tyburn beguiles,*
>
> *So well as a draught from the Bowl of Saint Giles!*

III.

There MULSACK and SWIFTNECK, both prigs from their birth,

OLD MOB and TOM COX took their last draught on earth :

There RANDAL, and SHORTER, and WHITNEY pulled up,

And jolly JACK JOYCE drank his finishing cup!

> *For a can of ale calms*
>
> *A highwayman's qualms,*
>
> *And makes him sing blithely his dolorous psalms!*
>
> *For nothing the transit to Tyburn beguiles,*
>
> *So well as a draught from the Bowl of St. Giles!*

IV.

When gallant Tom Sheppard to Tyburn was led,

" Stop the cart at the Crown—stop a moment," he said ;

He was offered the Bowl, but he left it and smiled,

Crying " Keep it till called for by Jonathan Wild !

> *" The rascal one doy*
>
> *Will pass by this way,*
>
> *And drink a full measure to moisten his clay !*
>
> *And never will Bowl of St. Giles have beguiled*
>
> *Such a thorough-paced scoundrel as* Jonathan Wild !"*

V.

Should it e'er be *my* lot to ride backwards that way,

At the door of the Crown I will certainly stay ;

I'll summon the landlord—I'll call for the Bowl,

And drink a deep draught to the health of my soul !

> *Whatever may hap,*
>
> *I'll taste of the tap,*
>
> *To keep up my spirits when brought to the crap !*
>
> *For nothing the transit to Tyburn beguiles,*
>
> *So well as a draught from the Bowl of St. Giles !*

THE NEWGATE STONE.[1]

I.

When Claude du Val was in Newgate thrown,
He carved his name on the dungeon stone ;
Quoth a dubsman, who gazed on the shattered wall,
" You have carved your epitaph, Claude du Val,

With your chisel so fine, tra la !"

II.

Du Val was hanged, and the next who came
On the selfsame stone inscribed his name ;
" Aha!" quoth the dubsman, with devilish glee,
" Tom Waters, *your* doom is the triple tree !

With your chisel so fine, tra la !"

[1] Set to music by Mr. G. Herbert Rodwell.

III.

Within that dungeon lay CAPTAIN BEW,

RUMBOLD and WHITNEY—a jolly crew!

All carved their names on the stone, and all

Share the fate of the brave DU VAL!

With their chisel so fine, tra la!

IV.

Full twenty highwaymen blithe and bold,

Rattled their chains in that dungeon old:

Of all that number there 'scaped not one

Who carved his name on the Newgate Stone,

With his chisel so fine, tra la!

THE CARPENTER'S DAUGHTER.

I.

THE carpenter's daughter was fair and free—

Fair, and fickle, and false was she!

She slighted the journeyman (meaning *me !*)

And smiled on a gallant of high degree.

     Degree! degree!

She smiled on a gallant of high degree.

II.

When years were gone by, she began to rue

Her love for the gentleman (meaning *you !*),

"I slighted the journeyman fond," quoth she,

"But where is my gallant of high degree?

     Where? where?

Oh! where is my gallant of high degree?"

OWEN WOOD.

I.

Once on a time, as I've heard tell,

In Wych-street, Owen Wood did dwell;

A carpenter he was by trade,

And money, I believe he made.

With a foodle doo!

II.

This carpenter he had a wife,

The ceaseless torment of his life;

Who, though she did her husband scold,

Loved well a woollen-draper bold.

With a foodle doo!

III.

Now Owen Wood had one fair child,

Unlike her mother, meek and mild;

Her love the draper strove to gain.

But she repaid him with disdain.

With a foodle doo !

IV.

In vain he fondly urged his suit,

And, all in vain, the question put;

She answered,—" Mr. William Kneebone,

Of me, sir, you shall never be bone."

With a foodle doo !

V.

" Thames Darrell has my heart alone,

A noble youth, e'en *you* must own:

And, if from him my love could stir,

Jack Sheppard I should much prefer."

With a foodle doo !

KING FROG AND QUEEN CRANE.

Old King Frog, he swore begar!

    Croakledom cree!—croakledom croo!

That he with Queen Crane would go to war,

    Blusterem boo!—thrusterem through!

With that, he summon'd his fiercest Frogs,

With great cock'd hats, and with queues like logs,

And says he, "Thrash these Cranes, you ugly dogs!

    Sing, Ventre-saint-gris!—Parbleu!"

To fight they went; but alack! full soon,

    Croakledom cree!—croakledom croo!

Messieurs the Frogs they changed their tune,

    Of blusterem boo!—thrusterem through!

For Queen Crane had a leader stout and strong,

With a bill like a fire-spit, six feet long,

And the Froggies he gobbled up all day long,

With their " Ventre-saint-gris !—Parbleu !"

MARLBROOK TO THE WARS IS COMING.

MARLBROOK to the wars is coming !

I fancy I hear his drumming ;

'Twill put an end to the mumming

  Of our priest-ridden Monarque !

For the moment he enters Flanders,

He'll scare all our brave commanders,

They'll fly like so many ganders,

  Disturb'd by a mastiff's bark.

He comes ; and at SCHELLENBERG licks 'em,

At BLENHEIM next, how he kicks 'em,

And on RAMILIES' plain how he sticks 'em

  With bay'net to the ground !

For, says he, " Those saucy Mounseers,

I'll thoroughly—thoroughly trounce, sirs,

As long as there's an ounce, sirs,

  Of powder to be found.

Now he's gone home so jolly,

And we're left melancholy,

Lamenting of our folly

 That such a part we took.

For bitterly has he drubb'd us,

And cruelly has he snubb'd us,

And against the grain has rubb'd us,

 This terrible Turk, MARLBROOK.

We hope he will never come back, sirs,

Our generals to attack, sirs,

And thrash them all in a crack, sirs,

 As he has done before.

But in case QUEEN ANNE should send him,

We trust she'll kindly lend him

Some Tories[1] to attend him,

 Then he'll return no more!

---

[1] It will be remembered that the Tories of those days were pretty nearly the Whigs of ours; and violently opposed to Marlborough, and the war with France.

THE BOOTS OF MARLBROOK.

I.

FOUR marshals of France vow'd their monarch to guard,

Bragging BOUFFLERS, vain VILLARS, VILLEROY, and TALLARD;

These four gasconaders in jest undertook

To pull off the boots of the mighty MARLBROOK.

                Brush—brush away!

II.

The field was first taken by BOUFFLERS and VILLARS,

But though they were the chaffers, yet we were the millers;

BONN, LIMBURGH, and HUY, soon our general took,—

'Twas not easy to pull off the boots of MARLBROOK.

                Brush—brush away!

·III.

TALLARD next essayed with BAVARIA's Elector,

But the latter turn'd out an indifferent protector;

For he SCHELLENBERG lost, while at BLENHEIM both shook

In their shoes, at the sight of the boots of MARLBROOK,

> Brush—brush away!

IV.

To RAMILIES next came the vaunting VILLEROY,

In his own esteem equal to Hector of Troy;

But he found, like the rest, that his man he mistook—

And fled at the sight of the boots of MARLBROOK.

> Brush—brush away!

V.

Then here's to the boots, made of stout English leather,

Well soled, and well heel'd, and right well put together!

He deserves not the name of a Briton, who'd brook

A word 'gainst the fame of the boots of MARLBROOK!

> Brush—brush away!

VI.

Of Gallia the dread, and of Europe the wonder,

These boots, like their master, will never knock under;

We'll bequeath 'em our sons, and our sons' sons shall look

With pride and delight on the boots of MARLBROOK.

Brush—brush away !

A YEAR AND A DAY.

I.

A YEAR and a Day is the period named

When, according to Custom, the FLITCH may be claimed;—

Provided the parties can swear and can prove,

They have lived the whole time in true conjugal love.

II.

'Tis a very old Custom of ours at Dunmow,—

Fitzwalter established it ages ago:

Its antiquity, sure, can be doubted by no man,

Since 'tis mentioned by Chaucer, and trusty Piers Plowman.

III.

That it is a good Custom, as well as an old,—

Our custom of Dunmow—you needn't be told—

A prize matrimonial—claim it we may—

Nell and I have been married a Year and a Day.

A YEAR AND A DAY.

(Jonas and Nelly Nettlebed.)

IV.

With all the conditions we've duly complied—

And our love and fidelity well have been tried:

Kneeling down at the Church-door, we dare to confess

That not e'en in thought, did we ever transgress.

V.

No woman, save Nell, has attractions for me;

And as I feel, I needn't assure you, feels she:

No man in the world, be he ever so big,

Can say Nelly cares for his nonsense a fig.

VI.

I'm a pattern to husbands, as she is to wives—

We teach all transgressors to alter their lives.

We show how much better it is to be true,

Than each other neglect, as some married folks do.

VII.

In short, we're as happy as couple can be,—

No long curtain lectures sweet Nell reads to me;

By no silly squabbles are we ever put out,

Nor do I ever scold, nor does she ever pout.

VIII.

As to wishing that we were unmarried again,—

A notion so stupid ne'er enter'd our brain :—

Far rather,—we give you our honour,—we would

Be married twice over again, if we could !

IX.

Three times did I marry the FLITCH to obtain—

Three times unsuccessful—the fourth time I gain :

Blest with Nelly, sweet Nelly, they can't say me nay,—

We've not had a wrong word for a Year and a Day !

THE BALLAD OF THE BEARD.

I.

In masculine beauty, or else I am wrong,

Perfection consists in a beard that is long;

By man it is cherished, by woman revered,—

Hence every good fellow is known by his beard.

II.

Barbarossa, and Blackbeard, and Bluebeard, we know,

Let the hair on their chins most abundantly grow:

So did Francis the First, and our Harry the bluff,

And the great Bajazet had beard more than enough.

III.

Now the faces of those bearded worthies compare

With the faces of others divested of hair;

And you'll very soon see—if you've got any eyes—

On which side the superiority lies.

IV.

Then take to the BEARD, and have done with the razor!

Don't disfigure yourself any longer, I pray, sir!

Wear a Beard.   You will find it becoming and pleasant,

And your wife will admire you much more than at present.

V.

Of cuts we've the Spanish, Italian, and Dutch,

The old and the new, and the common o'ermuch;

You may have your beard trimm'd any way that you please,

Curled, twisted, or stuck out like chevaux-de-frise.

VI.

You may wear, if you choose, a beard, pick-a-devant,

A beard like a hammer, or jagg'd like a saw,—

A beard called " cathedral," and shaped like a tile,

Which the widow in Hudibras served to beguile.

VII.

A beard like a dagger—nay, don't be afraid,—

A beard like a bodkin, a beard like a spade;

A beard like a sugar-loaf, beard like a fork,

A beard like a Hebrew, a beard like a Turk.

VIII.

Any one of these beards may be yours if you list—

According to fancy you trim it or twist.

As to colour, that matters, I ween, not a pin—

But a bushy black beard is the surest to win.

IX.

So take to the BEARD, and abandon the razor!

Have done with all soaping and shaving, I say, sir!

By a scrub of a barber be never more sheared, sir;

But adorn cheek and chin with a handsome long beard, sir!

OLD GRINDROD'S GHOST.[1]

I.

OLD GRINDROD was hanged on a gibbet high,

On the spot where the dark deed was done;

'Twas a desolate place, on the edge of a moor,—

A place for the timid to shun.

II.

Chains round his middle, and chains round his neck,

And chains round his ankles were hung:

And there in all weathers, in sunshine and rain,

Old Grindrod, the murderer, swung.

[1] Founded on an incident, related to me, with admirable humour, by my old and much-valued friend, GILBERT WINTER, late of Stocks, Manchester.

III.

Old Grindrod had long been the banquet of crows,

Who flocked on his carcase to batten;

And the unctuous morsels that fell from their feast

Served the rank weeds beneath him to fatten!

IV.

All that's now left of him is a skeleton grim,

The stoutest to strike with dismay;

So ghastly the sight, that no urchin, at night,

Who can help it, will pass by that way.

V.

All such as had dared, had sadly been scared,

And soon 'twas the general talk,

That the wretch in his chains, each night took the pains,

To come down from the gibbet—*and walk !*

VI.

The story was told to a Traveller bold,

At an inn, near the moor, by the Host;

He appeals to each guest, and its truth they attest,

But the Traveller laughs at the Ghost.

VII.

" Now, to show you," quoth he, " how afraid I must be,

　　A rump and a dozen I'll lay ;

That before it strikes One, I will go forth alone,

　　Old Grindrod a visit to pay.

VIII.

" To the gibbet I'll go, and this I will do,

　　As sure as I stand in my shoes ;

Some address I'll devise, and if Grinny replies,

　　My wager, of course, I shall lose."

IX.

" Accepted the bet ; but the night it is wet,"

　　Quoth the Host.　" Never mind !" says the Guest ;

" From darkness and rain, the adventure will gain,

　　To my mind an additional zest."

X.

Now midnight had toll'd, and the Traveller bold

　　Set out from the inn, all alone ;

'Twas a night black as ink, and our friend 'gan to think,

　　That uncommonly cold it had grown.

XI.

But of nothing afraid, and by nothing delayed;

  Plunging onward through bog and through wood;

Wind and rain in his face, he ne'er slackened his pace,

  Till under the gibbet he stood.

XII.

Though dark as could be, yet he thought he could see

  The skeleton hanging on high;

The gibbet it creaked; and the rusty chains squeaked;

  And a screech-owl flew solemnly by.

XIII.

The heavy rain pattered, the hollow bones clattered,

  The Traveller's teeth chattered—with cold—not with fright;

The wind it blew lustily, piercingly, gustily;

  Certainly not an agreeable night!

XIV.

"Ho! Grindrod, old fellow!" thus loudly did bellow,

  The Traveller mellow,—"How are ye, my blade?"—

"I'm cold and I'm dreary; I'm wet and I'm weary;

  But soon I'll be near ye!" the Skeleton said.

XV.

The grisly bones rattled, and with the chains battled,

　The gibbet appallingly shook ;

On the ground something stirr'd, but no more the man heard,—

　To his heels, on the instant, he took.

XVI.

Over moorland he dashed, and through quagmire he plashed ;

　His pace never daring to slack ;

Till the hostel he neared, for greatly he feared

　Old Grindrod would leap on his back.

XVII.

His wager he lost, and a trifle it cost ;

　But that which annoyed him the most,

Was to find out too late, that certain as fate,

　The Landlord had acted the Ghost.

THE BARBER OF RIPON AND THE GHOSTLY BASIN.

A TALE OF THE CHARNEL HOUSE.

I.

Since Ghost-Stories you want, there is one I can tell
Of a wonderful thing that Bat Pigeon befel:
A Barber, at Ripon, in Yorkshire was he,
And as keen in his craft as his best blade could be.

II.

Now Bat had a fancy,—a strange one, you'll own,—
Instead of a brass bowl to have one of bone:
To the Charnel-house 'neath the old Minster he'd been,
And there, 'mongst the relics, a treasure had seen.

III.

'Mid the pile of dry bones that encumber'd the ground,

One pumpkin-like skull with a mazard he found;

If home that enormous old sconce he could take,

What a capital basin for shaving 'twould make!

IV.

Well! he got it, at last, from the Sexton, his friend,

Little dreaming how queerly the business would end:

Next, he saw'd off the cranium close to the eyes;

And behold then! a basin capacious in size.

V.

As the big bowl is balanced 'twixt finger and thumb,

Bat's customers all with amazement are dumb;

At the strange yellow object they blink and they stare,

But what it can be not a soul is aware!

VI.

Bat Pigeon, as usual to rest went that night:

But he soon started up in a terrible fright:

Lo! giving the curtains and bedclothes a pull,

A Ghost he beheld—*wanting half of its skull!*

VII.

"Unmannerly barber!" the Spectre exclaimed;

"To desecrate bonehouses art not ashamed?

Thy crown into shivers, base varlet, I'll crack,

Unless, on the instant, my own I get back!"

VIII.

"There it lies on the table!" Bat quakingly said;

"Sure a skull cannot matter when once one is dead."—

"Such a skull as thine may not, thou addlepate fool!

But a shaver of clowns for a Knight is no rule!"

IX.

With this, the wroth Spectre its brainpan clapp'd on,

And holding it fast, in a twinkling was gone;

But ere through the keyhole the Phantom could rush,

Bat perceived it had taken the soap and the brush.

X.

When the Sexton next morn went the Charnel-house round,

The great Yellow Skull[1] in its old place he found:

And 'twixt its lank jaws, while they grinningly ope,

As in mockery stuck, are the Brush and the Soap!

[1] This ghostly relic may still be seen in the curious Charnel-house of Ripon Minster. The legend connected with it is devoutly believed by the Sexton, its narrator.

Translations.

ELEGY

ON THE

CARDINAL CARLO BORROMEO.[1]

WITH black funereal robe, and tresses shorn,
  O'erwhelmed with grief, sad Elegy appears;
And, by her side, sits Ecloga forlorn,
  Blotting each line she traces with her tears.

'Twas night!—long pondering on my secret woes,
  The third hour broke upon my vigil lone;
Far from my breast had sorrow chased repose,
  And fears presageful threatened ills unknown.

[1] Freely translated from the Latin of the Admirable Crichton.

Slumber, at length, my heavy eyelids sealed;
   The self-same terrors scared me as I slept:
Portentous dreams events to come revealed,
   And o'er my couch fantastic visions swept.

Upon the shoreless sea methought I sailed,
   No helmsman steered the melancholy bark;
Around its sides the pitying Nereids wailed
   Cleaving with snow-white arms the waters dark.

Cydippe, dolphin-borne, Ephyra fair,
   And Xanthia leave their halcyon-haunted caves,
With Doris and Cymodece to share
   The maddening strife of storm-awaken'd waves.

Drawn unresisting, where the whirling gyre
   Vexes the deep, the ship her prow inclines;
While, like a pharos' gleam, the lightning's fire
   Over the raging vortex redly shines.

Mix'd with the thunder's roar that shakes the skies,

   Notus and Africus and Boreas sound ;

Black wreathing clouds, like shadowy legions, rise,

   Shrouding the sea in midnight gloom profound.

Disabled, straining, by the tempest lashed,

   Reft of her storm-tried helmsman's guiding hand,

The vessel sinks!—amid the surges dashed,

   Vainly I struggle—vainly cry for land!

Alas! stern truths with dreams illusive meet!

   Latium the shipwreck of her hopes deplores!

The pious leader of the Insubrian fleet

   I mourn—a wandering Scot from Northern shores!

Weep youths! weep aged men! weep! rend your hair!

   Let your wild plaints be on the breezes tost!

Weep virgins! matrons! till your loud despair

   Outbraves her children's wail for Ilion lost!

In that wreck'd bark the Ship of Christ behold !

In its lost chief the Cardinal divine,

Of princely Lombard race ;[1] whose worth untold

Eclipsed the lofty honours of his line.

His suffering countrymen to rule, sustain,

By the All-wise was BORROMEO given ;

And he, who stoop'd not dignity to gain,[2]

Derived his high investiture from heaven.

[1] Saint Carlo Borromeo was born at Arona, near the Lago Maggiore, the loveliest of Italian lakes, on the 2nd of October, 1538. His family was, and still continues to be, the most illustrious in Lombardy. It derives, however, its proudest distinction from its connexion with the virtuous cardinal and his exalted nephew Frederigo, whose sublime character has been of late so exquisitely portrayed by Manzoni. If ever man deserved canonization, it was the subject of this elegy, whose whole life was spent in practices of piety ; and whose zeal, munificence, wisdom, toleration, and beneficence, have conferred lasting benefits on his creed and country.

[2] He was made Cardinal and Archbishop in his twenty-third year by his uncle, Pius VI., who had resigned several rich livings to him twelve years before,—EUSTACE. *Classical Tour through Italy.*

Bright as the sun o'er all pre-eminent,

   Or Cynthia glittering from her star-girt throne,

The saintly CHARLES, on truths sublime intent,

   Amid the purple hierarchy shone.

The Christian fleet, devoid of helm and sail,[1]

   He mann'd and led where roughest billows roll;

And, though no more his virtues wide prevail,

   Their sacred influence spreads from pole to pole.

His was the providence that all foresees,

   His, the trust placed, unchangeably, above;

His, strict observance of his sires' decrees,

   Rapt adoration, and fear-chasten'd love.

[1] Borromeo found the diocese of Milan in the most deplorable state of disorder. But with a vigorous and unsparing hand he reformed all ecclesiastical abuses—"C'est ainsi," observes M. Tabauraud, the writer of his Life in the "Biog. Universelle," "que l'Eglise de Milan, tombée dans une espèce d'anarchie depuis quatrevingts ans que ses archevêques n'y résidaient pas, reçut en peu d'années cette forme admirable qui, par la vie toute angélique de son clergé, la rendit le modèle de toutes les autres Eglises. Tant de réformes ne purent se faire sans de grands obstacles, qu'il surmonta par sa fermeté, sa patience et son imperturbable charité."

The faith in practice, not profession, shown,

    Which borrows all its glory from on high

Was his:—nor did his holiness, alone,

    Consist in outward forms of sanctity.

A willing ear unto the nobly-born,

    Nobler himself, he ne'er refused to yield;

Nor, Jesus' meek disciple, did he scorn

    The humble prayer that to his heart appealed.[1]

No dearer recollection than his name

    Bequeathed us, can unite him with the earth:

Nor can my praise add lustre to his fame—

    Proud heritage of unexampled worth![2]

[1] So unbounded was Borromeo's charity, that he sold his principality of Oria, and distributed the proceeds amongst the poor.

[2] The private virtues of Saint Charles, that is, the qualities which give true sterling value to the man, and sanctify him to the eyes of his Creator —I mean humility, self-command, temperance, industry, prudence, and fortitude—were not inferior to his public endowments. His table was for his guests; his own diet was confined to bread and vegetables; he allowed himself no amusement or relaxation, alleging that the variety of his

When, o'er his desolated city fell

The livid plague's inexorable breath,

Oft, in the lazzaretto's tainted cell,

Fervent, he prayed beside the couch of death.[1]

As through the fane the pale procession swept,[2]

Before its shrine he bent in lowliest wise

Imploring heaven, in mercy, to accept

His life, for them, a willing sacrifice.

duties was in itself a sufficient recreation. His dress and establishment were such as became his rank, but in private he dispensed with the attendance of servants, and wore an under dress, coarse and common; his bed was of straw; his repose short; and in all the details of life he manifested an utter contempt of personal ease and indulgence. —EUSTACE.

[1] During a destructive pestilence he erected a lazzaretto, and served the forsaken victims with his own hands.—EUSTACE.

[2] The incidents described in this and the following stanza do not occur in the original. As, however, they appear necessary to complete the picture of the holy Primate's career presented by the poem, I have ventured upon their introduction. These actions, as well as his heroic devotion to the plague-stricken in the lazzaretto, mentioned in the preceding verse, form subjects for part of the eight magnificent silver bas-reliefs which adorn the vaulted roof of the gorgeous subterranean chapel in the Duomo at Milan, where the body of the Saint reposes enshrined

When from the assassin's arm the bullet sped,

He blench'd not, nor his deep devotions stopt;

"*Be not dismay'd in heart!*"—the anthem said,

He rose—the bullet from his vestment dropt![1]

Not in the prism more varied hues reside,

Than bright examples in his course are traced :—

Alas! his longer sojourn here denied,

His guiding star is from its sphere effaced.

amid "barbaric pearl and gold." During the period of the plague, Borromeo was indefatigable in his exertions to arrest the terrible calamity. "Cherchant," says M. Tabauraud, "à désarmer la colère du ciel par des processions générales, auxquelles il assistait nu-pieds, la corde au cou, les yeux fixés sur son crucifix, qu'il arrosait de ses larmes, *en s'offrant à Dieu comme une victime de propitiation pour les péchés de son peuple!*"

[1] The ecclesiastical reformation effected by Saint Charles met, as was natural, with considerable opposition on the part of the corrupt and disorderly priesthood, and he became the object of their bitterest animosity. "Les plus opposés à la réforme," writes M. Tabauraud; "suscitèrent un frère *Farina*, qui se posta à l'entrée de la chapelle archiépiscopale où le Saint Prélat faisait sa prière avec toute sa maison; et, au moment où l'on chantait cette antienne; *Non turbetur cor vestrum neque formidet*, l'assassin, éloigné seulement de cinq ou six pas, tire un coup d'arquebuse sur Saint Charles, à genoux devant l'autel. A ce bruit, le chant cesse, la consternation est générale; le Saint, sans s'émouvoir, fait signe de continuer la prière: il se croyait cependant blessé mortellement, et offrait à Dieu le sacrifice de sa vie. *La prière finie, il se relève, et voit*

Alas! life's ebbing tide no hindrance knows!

  With man is nothing certain but to die!

Mortality, alone, presents a close

  Immutable, 'mid mutability.

As, in some stream remote, the swan expires,

  Breathing, unheard, her fate-foreboding strain,

So the declining Cardinal retires

  To steep Varalla's solitary fane.[1]

tomber à ses pieds la balle qu'on lui avait tirée dans le dos, et qui n'avait fait qu'effleurer son rochet."—BIOG. UNIVERSELLE. The holy primate endeavoured, ineffectually, to preserve Farina and the instigators of his crime from merited punishment. They were put to death, and Pius VI. dissolved the order (*Gli Umili*) to which they belonged.

[1] The Monastery of Monte Varalla is situated in the Piedmontese states, near the banks of the Sesia. Thither Saint Charles retired immediately previous to his dissolution, attended only by his confessor, the Jesuit Adorno,—and returned thence to Milan in a dying state. "Franciscum Adornum Societatis Jesu plurimi fecit qui cum in extremo vitæ curriculo per dies plurimos, quo tempore in Monte Varallo meditationibus se totum tradiderat CAROLUS ab ejus latere nunquam discesserit."— *Caroli Cardin. Borromæi Vita—Valerio.* ANTOINE GODEAU, *Bishop of Grasse,* who has written the life of the illustrious Primate, gives the following particulars of his melancholy visit to the Monastery:—" Encore que toute la vie de SAINT CHARLES fust une retraite mentale, toutefois il avait accoutumé d'en faire une locale tous les ans en quelque monastère

Like the fair flower that springs from winter's crust,

    Lombards! your Primate bursts his earthly chains;

And, in his Father's mansion with the Just,

    A portion and inheritance obtains.[1]

Within his chosen tomb calm may he sleep![2]

    Beatified, aloft, his spirit soars!

While Virtue's loss irreparable, deep,

    With reverential grief the Muse deplores.

écarté, où il employoit quelques jours pour faire une revue sévère de sa vie, et pour prendre un nouvel esprit de zèle et de piété. Avant que de s'en retourner à Milan, il voulut passer au *Mont Varalle*, dont nous avons parlé, et y faire ses exercices."—*Vie de S. Ch. Borromée. Liv. II. Ch. dernier.* M. MELLIN, in his "Voyage dans le Milanais," describing the mountain oratory of Varese, observes: "On va de là à *Varalle*, où les Histoires de l'Ancien et du Nouveau-Testament sont figurées dans cinquante-deux chapelles."

[1] The earthly pilgrimage of Saint Charles terminated on the 4th of November, 1584, at the age of forty-six years. He was canonized by Paul V., in 1610.

[2] "Cupiens hoc loco sibi monumentum vivens elegit."—*Epitaph inscribed, by his own desire, upon Borromeo's tomb.*

TO GASPAR VISCONTI.[1]

(CONGRATULATORY ADDRESS.)

When her fair land with grief o'erspread,

Insubria mourn'd her Primate dead;

When Borromeo to the tomb

Was borne 'mid all-pervading gloom;

When dimm'd with tears was every eye,

When breathed one universal sigh

The sorrowing lyre for him who slept,

I first—a Scottish minstrel—swept.

The night is pass'd, and dawn awakes,

Bright Cynthius through the vapour breaks,

[1] Freely translated from the Latin of the Admirable Crichton.

And Lucifer, with cheering beams,

From out his golden axle gleams.

Where late upon the raging sea

The wild winds rush'd tumultuously;

And the frail bark by surges tost,

Her tempest-braving helmsman lost,

Her timbers strain'd, her canvass riven,

Wide o'er the weltering waste was driven;

While her pale crew, with fear aghast,

Gazed (as they deem'd) on heaven their last!

With shrieks their hapless fate bewailing!

With prayers the threatening skies assailing!

—— A change is wrought!—hushed are the gales,

A soft and summer calm prevails;

And the glad ship in safety glides

Over the gently-rolling tides.

In troops o'er ocean's broad expanse

Day's rosy harbingers advance;

Bland Eolus careers the wave,

Fierce Notus hurries to his cave;

Young Titan from the waters springs,

With new-born lustre on his wings;

And over all things shines that sun,

Whose light a thousand vows have won.

Iŏ! with shouts the deck resound!

Iŏ! another chief is found!

Another leader hath been sent

To rule the Christian armament;

Whose firmness and undaunted zeal

Ensure uninterrupted weal:

Whose voice the Roman Rota sway'd,

Whose laws that synod sage obey'd;

Whose hand will guide with equal ease,

Religion's bark through stormy seas:

Whose power in exhortation shown,

Whose wisdom I myself have known;

When by his eloquence subdued,

In admiration lost, I stood.

Rejoice thrice-happy Lombardy!

That such a chief is given to thee!

A chief so free from aught of sin,

Virtue might be his origin :

Whose heavenly purpose, onward-tending,

Whose resolution calm, unbending,

Shall lead thee through the shades of night

To realms of everlasting light.

Haste Milanese! your Primate greet!

Prelates! your leader fly to meet!

Run maidens! youths! let each one bring

Some gift, some worthy offering!

Surrounding nations hail your choice,

Surrounding nations loud rejoice!

Like him, whom ye have lost, was none

Save him your choice has fall'n upon '

A father fond, a ruler wise,

GASPAR, in thee, we recognise :

Thy name, VISCONTI, seems to be

An earnest of prosperity.

To us thou art in our distress,

As manna in the wilderness.

Inhospitable Caucasus,

Sarmatian Boreas rigorous,

Seize on the caitiff, who denies

Thy all-acknowledg'd charities!

A glory art thou, and a star,

A light, a pharos seen afar!

And, clothed with majesty divine,

Shalt prove the pillar of thy line.

High rectitude and prescience

Are thine, and wide beneficence:

A Numa in thy sanctity,

A Cato in thy gravity,

Augustus in nobility.

Hence the High Pontiff Gregory,[1]

Who holds of Paradise the key,

For thee earth's chains hath cast aside,

For thee heaven's gate hath opened wide;

Milan's white robe hath round thee spread,

Her mitre placed upon thy head.

---

[1] Gregory XIII., the Pope by whom Gaspar Visconti was appointed to the Archiepiscopal see of Milan.

In thy blest advent all men see

Of peace a certain augury ;

All tongues are clamorous in thy praise,

All prayers are for thy length of days.

Amid the crowd, I, CRICHTON, born

On Caledonian shores forlorn,

Not all unknown, congratulate

Thee, GASPAR, on thine honour'd state.

Perpetual happiness be thine !

Thy bright, approving smile be mine :

Nor let thy taste, severe, disdain,

Primate, this welcome-breathing strain.

The Combat of the Thirty.

FROM A BRETON LAY OF THE FOURTEENTH CENTURY.

The Combat of the Thirty.

FROM A BRETON LAY OF THE FOURTEENTH CENTURY.

INTRODUCTION.

THE authenticity of the Combat of the Thirty, beyond doubt the most remarkable episode of the civil wars that desolated Brittany during the fourteenth century, was long disputed by both French and English historians, who seemed to regard the engagement as apocryphal. Yet there was no just reason for such doubts. The question, however, has been finally set at rest by the discovery of the ancient and almost contemporary Ballad, of which I have attempted the following version; and by the recovery of a missing chapter of Froissart, supplying details of the affair. The manuscript of the old Ballad was found in the Bibliothèque du Roi, by MM. de Freminville and Penhouët, the former of whom published an incorrect edition of it at Brest in 1819. A second and beautifully-printed edition, which left nothing to desire on the score of accuracy—the proofs having been collated word for word with the original manuscript by M. Méon—was brought out in 1827, by M. Crapelet, under the auspices of the Comte de Corbière, Minister of the Interior. More recently, the zeal and antiquarian learning of M. Pitre Chevalier, the author of "Ancient and Modern Brittany," have been devoted to the illustration of this curious historical poem, which he is willing to regard as the testimony of an almost eye-witness of the conflict, while he even ranks it above the newly-restored chapter of Froissart, as more "simple and characteristic, more complete and impartial." Indeed, with an enthusiasm excusable in a "Breton de la Bretagne bretonnante," he terms it a "*trésor sans prix*."

The new chapter of Froissart, to which I shall now advert, was discovered amongst the manuscript collections of the Prince de Soubise, and was published, in 1824, by the finder, M. Buchon, in his *Chroniques nationales et étrangères*. As this very interesting historical morceau has not, that I am aware, been included in any English edition of the old chronicler, or ever been translated into our language, I propose to give it entire.

How Messire Robert de Beaumanoir went forth to defy the Captain of Ploërmel, by name Brandebourg; and how he had a rude battle of Thirty against Thirty.

About this time, there occurred in Brittany a marvellous great feat of arms, which deserves to be had in remembrance, and to be held up as an encouragement and example to all bachelors. And to the end that you may the better understand it, you must know that there were continual wars in Brittany between the adherents of two noble dames,[1] in consequence whereof Messire Charles de Blois was made prisoner. Now the war was conducted by the adherents of the two dames by means of garrisons, which they maintained in castles and strong towns on either side. It chanced, one day, that Messire Robert de Beaumanoir, a

---

[1] "The Countess, at that time widow of Jean de Montfort, and Jeanne de Penthièvre, wife of Charles de Blois, who had been made prisoner at the battle of Roche-Derrien. These two heroines placed themselves at the head of their husbands' partisans, in defence of their respective rights. The war of succession of Jean III. lasted more than twenty years. Begun in 1341, it was only ended in 1364, by the Battle of Auray, at which Charles de Blois was killed by an English soldier, after performing prodigies of valour."—*Note in the Edition of the "Combat des Trente," published in* 1827.

valiant knight, and of the highest lineage in Brittany, and who was, moreover, governor of a castle called Castle Josselin, and had with him great store of men-at-arms of his kin, and other mercenaries, went forth to the town and castle of Ploërmel, the captain whereof was named Brandebourg, and had with him great store of German mercenaries, Englishmen, and Bretons, and belonged to the party of the Countess of Montfort. Now the afore-mentioned Messire Robert and his men rode nigh unto the barriers, and would fain have seen some one come forth to them. But no one issued out.

When Messire Robert beheld this, he drew yet nearer, and commanded the captain to be called. Hereupon, the captain come forth to speak with Messire Robert, assurances of safe-guard being given on either side. Then, said Messire Robert, "Brandebourg, have you no men-at-arms within, yourself or others, some two or three of you, who would like to joust with spear and sword against three others for love of their friends?" Brandebourg made answer and said: "My friends do not desire to be slain ingloriously in a single joust, for that would be a trial of fortune without result, and we should gain rather the name of rashness and folly than reap renown, honour, and reward. But I will tell you what we will do, an you list. You shall take from your garrison twenty or thirty of your fellowship, and I will take the like number from mine. Then let us repair to an open plain, where none can hinder or disturb us, and give orders, on pain of the halter, to our companions on either side, as well as to all beholders, that they shall not render aid or comfort to any combatant. This done, we will make proof of our prowess, and so do that they shall speak of us hereafter in halls, palaces, and other places throughout the world. And may fortune and honour befal those for whom God hath destined them."

"By my fay," said Messire Robert de Beaumanoir, "you speak bravely. I agree. Therefore, be you thirty, and we will be thirty likewise; for thus I promise it on my knightly faith."

"Thus also do I promise it," answered Brandebourg, "for by this means more honour will be acquired, and maintained, than by a joust."

Thus was the affair plighted and settled. The day was fixed for the Wednesday then after, being the fourth day from the defiance. In the interval, each chose his thirty men, as seemed good to him, and all the sixty provided themselves with arms fitted for the occasion.

When the day was come, the thirty companions of Brande-bourg heard mass, after which they armed themselves, and repaired to the spot where the battle was to take place. Dismounting from their horses, they forbade all such as weie there to interfere in case mischance befel them or their companions; and thus likewise did the companions of the Baron de Beaumanoir. Now these thirty companions, whom we shall call Englishmen, had tarried long for the others, whom we shall style Frenchmen. When the thirty Frenchmen were come, they dismounted, and gave the orders to their companions, as before related. Some say that five of their number remained at the entrance of the place of combat, while twenty-five dismounted, as the English had done. When the sixty were drawn up in front of each other, they parleyed together for a short time, and then retired on either hand, and made all those who were looking on with-draw to a distance. Then one of them gave the signal, and they rushed together at once, fighting stoutly in a heap, and gene-rously rescuing one another when they saw their companions in danger.

Soon after they came together thus, one of the Frenchmen was killed, but this did not prevent the others from fighting, but the combat was maintained right valiantly on both sides, as if they had been so many Rolands and Olivers. I cannot say for truth "if these or those did best," neither can I fairly place one above the other; but all fought so long that they completely lost strength and breath. Being compelled to stop and repose themselves awhile, a truce was proclaimed, which was to last until they had rested sufficiently, when the first who should arise was to summon the others. There were found dead four Frenchmen and two Englishmen. They rested for a long time on either side, and such as could obtain it drank wine, which was brought them in bottles, then braced up their battered armour, and dressed their wounds.

When they were thus refreshed, the first who arose gave the signal, and recalled the others. Then began again the combat as furiously as before, and it lasted for a long while. The combatants had swords from Bordeaux, short and stiff, pikes and daggers, and some had axes, wherewith they gave each other marvellously great blows. And some grappled with their foes in the strife, and smote them and spared them not. You may well believe that amongst them there was many a fine feat of arms; set as they were man to man, body to body, hand to hand. Not for a hundred years has been heard of the like.

Thus they fought like good champions, and very valiantly

maintained this second attack. But in the end the English had the worst of it. For, as I have heard tell, one of the Frenchmen, who remained on horseback, broke their ranks and trampled them under foot without difficulty, so that Brandebourg, their captain, and eight of his companions, were then slain; and the others, seeing that they could neither defend them nor lend them aid, surrendered themselves prisoners, for they could not, and would not fly. And the aforesaid Messire Robert, and such of his fellowship as were left alive, took them and conducted them to Josselin Castle as their prisoners, and afterwards allowed them ransom courteously, when their hurts were healed, for there was not one amongst them, French or English, who was not grievously wounded. Sithence, I saw, seated at the table of Charles, King of France,[1] a Breton knight, who had been present at the conflict, Messire Yervains (Yves) Charruel; his visage was so gashed and hacked that it showed plainly enough that the affair had been well fought. There also I saw Messire Enguerrant Duedins, a good knight of Picardy, who gave like proof that he had been at the fight; and another esquire, named Hues de Raincevaus. So this action came to be much talked

---

[1] Charles V., surnamed the Wise, who ascended the throne in 1364.

about. By some it was looked upon as of little account, by others as a marvellous feat, and of great hardihood.

Froissart's account of the combat, as will be seen, corresponds in a great measure with the description of the engagement given in the ballad; but the old chronicler says that the day appointed was the Wednesday after the defiance, whereas the writer of the lay fixes it, with great precision, upon Saturday, the vigil of Sunday, *Lætare Jerusalem*. Froissart also makes no mention of the most noticeable incident in the combat; namely, the stern rebuke administered by Geoffroy du Bois to the Breton leader, when the latter, athirst and bleeding, cried out for drink—"Drink thy own blood, Beaumanoir, thy thirst will pass away." The old chronicler's description of Yves Charruel's slashed visage is very striking; but the names of Enguerrant Duedins and Hues de Raincevaus do not appear in the list of combatants given by other historians.

Mr. Weld, in his pleasant *Vacation in Brittany*, says that, "according to tradition, Beaumanoir, though severely wounded and wearied, slew no less than five Englishmen with his own hands." But this wondrous display of prowess on the part of the Baron is not supported by more authentic narratives of the fight. On the contrary, the real hero of the day on the Breton side, though the palm of valour was adjudged to the Sire de Tinténiac, was Guillaume de Montauban. But for Montauban's device, the English, under the guidance of Croquart, would un-questionably have come off the victors. This stout German mercenary, the winner of the prize of valour on the English side, was taken with the other prisoners to Josselin, and subsequently released. Froissart devotes a chapter to him (chap. cxlviii.), and thus winds up his history: "King John of France made him the offer of knighting him, and marrying him very richly, if he would quit the English party, and promised to give him two thousand livres a year ; but Croquart would never listen to it. It chanced one day, as he was riding a young horse, which he had just purchased for three hundred crowns, and was putting him to his full speed, that the horse ran away with him, and, in leap-ing a ditch, stumbled into it, and broke his master's neck. Such was the end of Croquart."

Of the chivalrous Marshal de Beaumanoir, the friend and com-panion-at-arms of the renowned Bertrand du Guesclin, the cha-racter is thus summed up by a French writer: "In his long career, illustrated by important embassies and difficult commands, he was ever remarkable for loyalty and courage ; but his first title to glory is having been the leader of the Bretons at the Combat of the Thirty."

Concerning the English leader, Sir Robert Bembrough (Bembro, or Brandebourg, as he is indifferently styled), nothing can be discovered ; except that at the death of the brave Sir Thomas d'Agworth ("the English Achilles," as M. Pitre Chevalier terms him, "who covered himself with glory, by resisting with a handful of men the whole army of Charles de Blois"), he was appointed by Montford and Edward III. to the command of the garrison at Ploërmel, where he practised great cruelties upon the unfortunate Bretons.

As it cannot fail to interest the reader, I will now cite the very accurate description of the locality of the memorable combat given by M. Pitre Chevalier in his *Bretagne Ancienne et Moderne :* "The traveller, proceeding from Ploërmel to Josselin, after quitting the smiling environs of the first-named town, enters upon an arid and vast moor, without verdure and without trees, covered with the wild heath of Armorica, which hardly sparkles beneath the brightest rays of the sun. In the centre of this moor, equidistant from the two towns, formerly stood the venerable oak that shaded the champions of Mi-Voie. Towards the end of the sixteenth century, this old witness of the combat of giants was thrown to the earth by the axe of the League. Soon afterwards a stone cross replaced the oak. Reared close by the roadside, it enjoined the passer-by to bare his head and pray. The cross was thrown down, firstly, in 1775; but at the request of M. Martin d'Aumont, the States of Brittany restored it, and engraved upon its base the following inscription, reported by Ogée:—

A LA MEMOIRE PERPETUELLE

DE LA BATAILLE DES TRENTE, QUE MONSEIGNEUR LE MARECHAL

DE BEAUMANOIR A GAGNEE EN CE LIEU

LE XXVII. MARS, L'AN MCCCL.

"The Revolution of 1793, not less brutal than the League, sought to destroy the remembrance of the Thirty with the mark whereby it was preserved. But the memorial was gloriously revived, while the Revolution itself perished.

"In 1811, the council of the arrondissement of Ploërmel demanded that a grant of 600 fr. should be dedicated to the erection of a monument in honour of the combatants of Mi-Voie. The council-general of Morbihan applauded the idea, and voted for the same object the sum of 2400 fr. On the 11th of July, 1819, the first stone was laid by the Comte de Coutard, lieutenant-general, commander of the thirteenth military division, by M. de Chazelles, Baron de Lunac, prefect of Morbihan, and by M. Pitou, chief engineer of the corps of Sappers and Miners. The benediction was pronounced by M. de Bausset Roquefort, Bishop of Vannes.

"This monument, which all may now see, is an obelisk fifteen metres high, one metre and sixty centimetres wide at the base, and one metre wide at the top. Composed of layers of granite, it occupies the centre of a plantation of pines and cypresses, the highest of which does not exceed a hundred and forty metres.

"On the eastern front may be read these words :

SOUS LE REGNE DE LOUIS XVIII.,

ROI DE FRANCE ET DE NAVARRE,

LE CONSEIL GENERAL DU DEPARTEMENT DU MORBIHAN A

ELEVE CE MONUMENT A LA GLOIRE DES XXX. BRETONS.

"The west front bears the same inscription in the Celtic language. On the south are engraved the names of the combatants; on the north the date of the combat, March 27th, 1351. Near the monument is placed the stone restored in 1775 by the States of Brittany. *Voilà tout.*"

M. Pitre Chevalier then proceeds to broach the notion of what he deems would constitute a fitting monument to the Thirty, and it must be owned that the conception is not devoid of grandeur. "In place of this needle of stone, which resembles everything and signifies nothing, dare to realise the dream of a Breton pilgrim. Take from the bowels of the 'land of granite' thirty gigantic blocks, such as are to be found at Carnac or at Lok-Mariaker. Peradventure, you may find them on the very moor which was bedewed with the blood of the Thirty. Range these blocks in line of battle upon the place of the combat, as were ranged the champions of Brittany before the Marshal de Beaumanoir. Summon thirty Breton artists, and, if artists are wanting, summon workmen; order these simple statuaries to carve from each block a colossal knight, with his helm on head, his hand upon his sword, and his shield by his side; all this to be naturally and largely indicated, as becomes men of iron sculptured in granite. Provided that the manly visage is distinguishable under the visor, that the outline of the human form is preserved, that the armour defines itself boldly against the sky, and that the pedestal and the statue form an indestructible mass, nothing more is wanted. Upon these thirty escutcheons engrave the thirty names and the thirty armorial bearings. Plant in the middle of the line an oak like that of Mi-Voie. Let it grow and spread itself out freely till it shall cover all the knights with its shade. And when, one day, the traveller crossing this moor shall see rising before him this enormous tree, and those thirty stone warriors, whether the sun may project afar their gigantic silhouettes, or the moon may multiply or render yet larger their phantoms, that traveller will recognise a nation which for three thousand years has repulsed the foreigner, and which yet knows how, like the ancient Druids, to erect memorial stones to its heroes."

It may be mentioned that among the signatures of those who were not present at the ceremony of laying the first stone of the pyramidal monument to the Thirty, but who desired to subscribe the procès verbal, occur the names of the Duc de Serent (the last descendant of Jean de Serent, one of the Thirty), who died in 1822, without issue; the Comte de Tinténiac, descendant of the renowned Sire de Tinténiac; the Comte du Parc and the Vicomte Maurice du Parc, descendants of Maurice du Parc, one of the Thirty.

So great was the impression produced by the Battle of Mi-Voie, that, for more than a century after its occurrence, in Britanny, France, and England, it was a common expression to say, in allusion to any gallant or terrible action, "They fought as they did at the Combat of the Thirty."

The memory of the famous combat, so dear to their national pride, is still fondly cherished by the Breton peasantry. To this day, Mr. Weld tells us, they chant its glories at their Pardons, in a ballad in the Cornouaille dialect, called "Stourm Ann Tregont." Mr. Weld also states that the same ballad was very generally sung by these sturdy peasants, to incite each other to valour, during the Chouan war.

Honour to the brave men, on either side, who fought by the Mid-Way Oak. Honour to those who fell. Honour to those who won. Honour to those who lost. Assuredly, we have no cause to be ashamed of our share in the Combat of the Thirty.

THE COMBAT OF THE THIRTY.

Here begins the Battle of Thirty Englishmen against Thirty Bretons, which took place in Brittany in the year of Grace One Thousand Three Hundred and Fifty, on Saturday, the Vigil of Sunday Lœtare Jerusalem.[1]

Fytte ye First.

The Defiance.

I.

SEIGNEURS, knights, barons, bannerets, and bachelors, I pray,
Bishops and abbots, holy clerks, heralds and minstrels gay,
Ye valiant men of all degrees, give ear unto my lay.
Attend, I say, and ye shall hear how Thirty Englishmen,
As lions brave, did battle give to Bretons three times ten.
And sith the story of this fight I shall tell faithfully,

[1] March 27, 1351.   (New Style.)

A hundred years hereafter it shall remembered be,

And warriors hoar recount it then to children on the knee.

·

II.

In stories where good precept with ensample ye unite,

All men of worth and wisdom take exceeding great delight ;

Only envious knaves and faitours treat such ditties with despite.

Wherefore, without further prelude, I will now the tale recite

Of the Combat of the Thirty—that most memorable fight !

Beseeching Christ, our blessed Lord, in whom we place our

     trust,

Pity to have on those who fought, sith most of them are dust.[1]

III.

Before the Castle of Aurai stout Daggeworth[2] had been slain,

Worsted in a rude encounter with the Barons of Bretaigne;

---

[1] Some of the Knights engaged in the Combat of Thirty were alive
when the author of the Lay wrote his Relation.

[2] "Sir Thomas Daggeworth" (styled Dagorne in the Lay) "was
appointed Commander in Brittany, by writ of privy seal, dated Reading,
January 10, 1347."—*Fœdera*. Daggeworth commanded the Castle of
Aurai for the Countess of Montfort. His defeat and death are thus
described by Froissart. "In the beginning of August in the year 1350,

But his death, as ye shall hear anon, proved a loss and not

    a gain.

For while he ruled within Aurai no tiller of the soil,

Nor any peaceful citizen the English mote despoil.

But when he fell, Bembrough[1] arose, a chief with iron hand,

Who Daggeworth's treaty broke straightway, and ravaged all

    the land.

" Now, by Saint Thomas !" Bembrough swore, "avenged shall

    Daggeworth be !

Such ingrate knaves as these to spare were sinful clemency."

And well he kept his ruthless vow, for when he took Ploërmel,

Small mercy did he show to those within his power who fell.

Raoul de Cahours and many other knights and squires, to the number of one hundred men-at-arms, or thereabouts, combated with the commander for the King of England in Brittany, called Sir Thomas Daggeworth, before the Castle of Aurai. Sir Thomas and all his men were slain, to the amount of about one hundred men-at-arms."

[1] Sir Robert Bembrough. The author of the Lay calls him Bomeboure, and the French chroniclers write the name indifferently Bembro and Brandebourg. It has been conjectured that it might be Pembroke. Ormerod, in his Memoir of Sir Hugh Calverley, referring to the Combat of the Thirty, states that " the English commander at Ploërmel is supposed to have been Sir Richard Greenacre, of Merlay."

Sore wasted he the country round, until that happy day

When Beaumanoir, the Baron good, to Ploërmel took his way ;

From Josselin Castle did he come to aid the hapless folk

Who groaned, unpitied, unrelieved, 'neath Bembrough's cruel
    yoke.

As Beaumanoir and his esquires the English camp drew nigh,

Full many a captive they beheld lamenting dolefully.

For some they saw chained hand and foot—some by the thumbs
    were tied,—

Together link'd by twos and threes—torment on every side.

IV.

When Beaumanoir and his esquires in Bembrough's presence
    stood,

Thus haughtily the mail-clad throng bespoke the Baron good.

"Ye knights of England, valiant sirs, I pray ye, list to me,

The helpless captive to maltreat is shame to chivalry.

And if the peaceful husbandman ye torture and ye kill,

Whom shall ye find your vines to dress—who will your granaries
    fill ?

Trust me, brave sirs, ye do great wrong, and there an end must be,

As ye do hope for grace yourselves, of this severity."

" Baron de Beaumanoir," quoth Bembrough, "hold your peace,

For till our conquest be assured, these things shall never cease.

Question thereon there must be none. Now, mark well what I say.

A noble duchy in Bretaigne Montfort shall have alway—

From Pontorson to Nantes—from Nantes to Saint Mahé.

This shall he have. But of all France crown'd king shall

    Edward be,

And so on every side extend our English mastery,

Maugre the boastful French, and their allies, perdy!"

Made answer then the Baron good, and stoutly thus did say—

" Songez un autre songe, messire, cestui est mal songé.

Not half a foot, Sir Robert, shall you advance that way.

A truce to idle taunts!—fanfaronades are naught,—

And those who loudest prate do least, as I've been taught.

'Twere best, methinks, adjust our difference in this way

By mortal combat in the field on some appointed day.

Thirty 'gainst Thirty, an you list, together we will fight,

With spear and sword, with axe and mawle,—and Heaven defend

    the right !"

" Now, by my soul!" cried Bembrough, "I heartily agree

Unto your terms, and as you fix the combat, it shall be ;—

Thirty 'gainst Thirty of the best of either company,—

And for the day—all days alike for fighting are to me!"

Whereat he turned him to his Knights, laughing disdainfully.

Then was the battle 'twixt them sworn, each plighting solemnly

His knightly word to use thereat no base superchery.

With one consent a day they named—it was the day before

Lætare[1] Sunday—when good men with gifts the altars store.

The Vigil of *Lætare* 'twas,—and would ye know the year ?—

Fifty to Thirteen Hundred add, and ye shall have it clear.

Now to the King of Glory let us offer earnest prayer,

That those who fight for truth and right, He have within His

    care !

v.

With lightened heart to Josselin did Beaumanoir return,

Eager he was that all his knights the enterprise should learn ,

---

[1] Mid-Lent Sunday, anciently called *Lætare Jerusalem*, because on that day the introit of the Mass begins with those words. "In the former days of superstition," says Brande, "while that of the Roman Catholics was the established religion, it was the custom for people to visit their Mother Church on Mid-Lent Sunday, and to make their offerings at the high altar."

And as the throng he thus bespoke, like fire their breasts did

    burn:

"Seigneurs and valiant knights, this day have I defied

Bembrough to meet me in the field—Thirty on either side—

And for companions in the fray we both may freely choose

Such as the lance and battle-axe, and dagger best can use.

Hence Thirty of the most expert amongst ye, sirs, I lack,

Proud Bembrough and his chosen men like bears and wolves to

    hack.

Trust me the fame of this emprise shall travel throughout France,

From Bourgoigne to the Switzer's land, from Milan to Plaisance.

How say ye, knights and barons bold ?—will ye not have it so ?"

With one accord they made reply—"Thirty with you shall go.

And when we meet them in the field these Englishmen shall feel

What weighty blows, and well applied, a Breton arm can deal.

Then choose the best amongst us, sir—Heaven grant good choice

    you make!"

"Gramercy!" cried De Beaumanoir, "Tinténiac[1] first I take,

---

[1] Two champions of this name fought on Beaumanoir's side—the Sire de Tinténiac and Alain. The Lord of Tinténiac obtained the prize of valour on the part of the Bretons.

Next Guy de Rochefort, Saint-Yvon, and good Yves Charruel.

Caron de Bosdegas be mine, with Robin Raguenel.

Jean Rousselot, Geoffroy Du Bois, and valorous Arrel,

My life upon it each of ye 'gainst Bembrough will fight well.

"Thus far my knights I've ta'en. Esquires I next must choose—

Guillaume de Montauban, I wot, my quest will not refuse?

Alain de Tinténiac I claim, Alain de Keranrais,

Olivier, uncle to the last, and you, De Fontenay?

Tristan de Pestivien, and Louis Goyon brave,

With Hugues Capus-le-Sage, sans question, I must have.

Young Geoffroy de la Roche full soon shall knighted be,

Whose valiant sire to fight the Turk[1] hath sailed across the sea.

Poulard, Beaucorps, Pontblanc, ye twain De Trisquidys,

Du Parc, Mellon, and De la Marche,—ye all must come with me.

Jean de Serent I call on you, and Guillaume de la Lande;

And with Pachard and Monteville I shall complete my band."

Now all, whom Beaumanoir did choose, returned him thanks

    straightway;

[1] Budes de la Roche, father of the warrior mentioned in the ballad,
fought at the Siege of Constantinople, and in Greece.

And for success upon their arms right fervently did pray.

Heaven guard them well!—and to their foes the disadvantage

   send,

That for Bretaigne the coming fight triumphantly may end!

VI.

Now turn we to the other side, and let us see what way

Haughty Sir Robert Bembrough chose his comrades for the fray.

Sir Robert Knolles[1] he first did take—next Sir Hugh Calverley,[2]

---

[1] "Sir Robert Knolles (called Robert Canoles in the Lay) was but of mean parentage in the county of Chester, but by his valour advanced from a common soldier in the French wars under Edward III. to a great commander. Being sent general of an army into France, in dislike of their power, he drove the people before him like sheep, destroying towns, castles, and cities, in such manner and number, that long after, in memory of this act, the sharp points and gable ends of overthrown houses and minsters were called Knolles's Mitres. After which, to make himself well-beloved of his country, he built a goodly fair bridge at Rochester, over the Medway, with a chapel and chauntry at the east end thereof. He built much at the Greyfriars, London, and a hospital at Rome for English travellers and pilgrims. He deceased at his manor of Scone Thorpe, in Norfolk—was buried by the Lady Constance his wife, in the Church of Greyfriars, London, 18th August, 1407."—*Weever's Funeral Monuments.* Sir Robert was created a Knight of the Garter by Richard II.

[2] This distinguished knight (Hue de Carualay, as he is styled in the

With Richard de la Lande—three better might not be.

Hervé de Lexualen came next, Walton and Bélifort,

The last-named giant knight an iron mallet bore,

Its weight was five and twenty pounds—yea, twenty-five and
    more !

His list of knights complete, proud Bembrough next essayed

Esquires the hardiest to find, and thus his choice he made.

John Plesington he fixed upon, Repefort, Le Maréchal,

Hérouart and Boutet d'Aspremont, the stoutest of them all.

Richard and Hugues, Le Gaillard named, Jennequin de Beton-
    champ,

All these he took, and lastly chose Hucheton de Clamaban.

Lay) was the eldest son of David Calverley (or Calveley), of Lea, in
Cheshire.   He first appeared as one of the combatants in the noted
conflict described in the Lay;   next at the Battle of Aurai, 1364;   then
as a captain of Free Companies in the service of Henry of Trastamare;
and after other exploits too numerous to particularise, he ended his
brilliant and adventurous career by founding a college at Bunbury, in
his native county.   "His body was interred in the chancel of his college,
where his armed effigy reposes on one of the most sumptuous altar-tombs
that his county can boast."—*Ormerod's Cheshire*.   It has been asserted,
but not proved, that Sir Hugh Calverley married a queen of Arragon.

De Clamaban a falchion had as sharp as any dart,

Wherewith he fought as legends tell of royal Agapart,

Each blow lopped off a head or limb, or pierced right to the heart.

For men-at-arms of valour proved, Bembrough need not search far,

Within the English camp, I trow, a hundred such there are ;

But he who holds the foremost place is resolute Croquart.

Next Gaultier Lallemant stands forth ; and Guillemin-le-Gaillard ;

Then Daggeworth, nephew to the chief, agile as is a pard ;[1]

Helcoq and Isannay come next, and Jennequin Taillard,

Dardaine, Adès, Troussel,[2] and Rango-le-Couart,

De Gannelon and Helichon, Vitart and Mélipart.

Such were the Thirty Combatants on Bembrough's side enrolled ;

'Midst them were twenty Englishmen, as Libyan lions bold,

Brabanters four, and Germans six ;—and thus the list is told.

[1] This young champion subsequently won his spurs, and as Sir Nicholas Daggeworth fought during the Siege of Rennes, in 1357, in single combat with the redoubted Bertrand du Guesclin. "The terms of the combat," according to Froissart, "were to be three courses with spears, three strokes with battle-axes, and three stabs with daggers. The two knights behaved most valiantly, and parted without hurting each other. They were seen with pleasure by both armies."

[2] Called John Russel, in the Histoire de Bretagne.

Furnished they were with habergeons, bacinets, and greaves, I
    ween,

And armed with falchion, lance and sword, war-axe and dagger
    keen.

To list their braggart talk would move the moodiest man to mirth,

Thirty to match them, it would seem, could not be found on earth.

By Christ, they sware, that Beaumanoir and his companions brave

To death were doomed, and all Bretaigne to Dinan they would
    have!

But Beaumanoir he boasted not, but reverently prayed

The mighty Ruler of Events a rightful cause to aid!

𝕱𝖞𝖙𝖙𝖊 𝖞𝖊 𝕾𝖊𝖈𝖔𝖓𝖉.

•

Of the Combat, and the great feats of arms done thereat.

I.

Now when the day appointed for the combat had arrived,

De Beaumanoir and all his knights by holy priests were shrived;

At early dawn they mass did hear, then to the altar led,

They knelt them down, and took the cup, and ate the sacred bread.

II.

" Good sirs," quoth lordly Beaumanoir, while marshalling his band,

Be of stout heart, and valiantly these Englishmen withstand.

And if Christ Jesus in his grace shall give us mastery,

Throughout the realm entire of France rejoicing there shall be ;

And Charles de Blois of Brittany,—Duke Charles the Debonair,—

He and his gracious Duchess Jeanne, valiant and wise as fair,—

Mine own right-noble kinswoman—great love for us shall bear

Then before God, the mighty God of Battles, let us swear,

That if proud Bembrough and his host we find in yonder plain,

Not one of all their lineage shall see their face again !"

III.

That morn, betimes, bold Bembrough, with his gallant company

Of thirty fearless combatants, unto the field did hie.

Now would ye know the spot whereon this famous fight befel,

Midway it lies 'twixt Josselin and the Castle of Ploërmel.

A solitary tree doth grow on the far-stretching plain,

Known as the Mid-Way Oak[1]—long may that mark remain !

When to the place of rendezvous proud Bembrough had drawn
    nigh,

Unto his thirty men-of-arms he thus spake boastfully :

" My magic books I've caused be read,[2] and Merlin unto me

Doth prophesy, upon this day, a signal victory.

[1] *Le Chesne den my voie, ainsi est son appel.*

[2] *J'ai fait lire mes livres.* " This expression," Mr. Weld remarks,
" is explained by the fact that the knights and gentry of the period
referred to in the poem were unable to read." But it may also imply
that the superstitious English leader, being unable to decipher the mystic
characters on his scrolls, caused them to be interpreted to him.

Be confident, then, valiant sirs, as well, I wot, ye may,

For of the host of Beaumanoir few shall survive the day.

And such as shall surrender in the combat I ordain

In his name, shall to Edward good, our sovran lord, be ta'en.

An earnest shall they be to him, that not alone Bretaigne

But all the realm of fertile France shall to his crown pertain!"

Thus spake Sir Robert Bembrough, thus spake he as he thought;

But if it please the King supreme with whom all kings are nought.

Things to a different issue far shall surely yet be brought.

IV.

As Bembrough and his company by the Mid-Way Oak did halt,

"Where art thou, Beaumanoir?" he cried, "I have thee at default;

Hadst thou been here full speedily discomfited thou'dst been."

E'en as the words fell from his lips De Beaumanoir was seen.

"Ho! Beaumanoir!" cried Bembrough, then, "good friends we yet may be,

If to adjourn this combat sworn we both of us agree;

License to fight from my liege lord, great Edward, I'll obtain.

And from the King of Saint-Denis, like license thou shalt gain.

This done, our compact we'll renew, and fix at once the day."[1]

"Counsel I'll take," quoth Beaumanoir, sternly, "on what you

    say."

V.

Without more words, the Baron good did to his men return,

And while he thus bespoke the throng, with wrath his cheeks

    did burn :

"How think ye, sirs ?" he scornful laughed, "Bembrough would

    have us go

Back from this field, where we have come to fight, without a

    blow.

He would adjourn the combat, sirs.   Speak ! will ye have it so ?

This hesitation on the part of Bembrough would appear, at first, to be irreconcilable with his previous address to his followers, as well as with his own subsequent conduct. But it seems to have occurred to him (somewhat too late his opponent thought) that the combat between himself and Beaumanoir, unauthorized by their respective sovereigns would be irregular, and ought, therefore, to be deferred till due license for it could be obtained.

For mine own part I swear to you—and Heaven the truth doth
    know!—
For all the treasure upon earth, I'd not the fight forego!"

Then out and spake Yves Charruel, with choler raging hot—
Betwixt the sea and where they stood a bolder knight was not:
"Sir, here are thirty men-at-arms have come unto this spot,
Tough spear, martel, and battle-axe, dagger and sword we've
    got;
Ready prepared we are to fight, and by Saint-Honoré!
With Bembrough and his fellowship we mean to fight to-day.
We mean to fight and vanquish those base braggarts, since they
    dare
Dispute the title of the land with the Duke Debonair.
Perish the dastard vile I say, who tamely would go back,
And when his foes before him stand, would not those foes
    attack!"

"Thou sayest well, Yves Charruel, to go back were foul scorn;
The combat we will have with them, even as it hath been
    sworn."

VI.

" Bembrough," quoth lordly Beaumanoir, as toward him he did
    turn,

" Hear what my brave companions say—thy offer they do spurn.

Shameful they hold 'twould be in us the combat to delay,

Which thou hast proffered Charles de Blois, through me and
    mine to-day.

We all have sworn, that in the sight of the Barons of Bretaigne,

Thou and thy fellowship this day shall shamefully be slain !"

"Tush, Beaumanoir," bembrough cried out, " mere folly thou
    wilt do,

And, when too late, thy rashness great full bitterly thou'lt rue.

For the flower of all thy duchy shall upon this plain be left,

And thy liege lord of his noblest and his bravest be bereft."

" Sir Robert," answered Beaumanoir, " I utterly deny,

That I unto this field have brought the flower of Brittany.

Rohan, Laval, and Lohéac, and Quentin are not here,

And many other noble knights of prowess without peer ;

But I have with me thirty men who nothing living fear

Thirty clean men-of-arms, who practise not treason or perfidy—

And all have sworn, ere compline-time, thou and thy host shall

    die!"

Then to him Bembrough answer made, laughing disdainfully:

" Less than a clove of garlic rank, proud lord, I value thee;

Thy fellowship I hold as cheap, and will have mastery.

All Brittany shall soon be ours, and eke all Normandy."

Then turning to his company, he shouted lustily,

" Upon them!—strike these Bretons down, and put them to the

    sword!

Spare none!—to work us deadly harm they all are of accord."

VII.

Unto their leaders' battle-cries loud shouts responsive rose,

Impatient were the sixty all from words to come to blows.

Like bolts unto the fray they rush; the shock is fierce and

    dread:

Yves Charruel is prisoner ta'en, Mellon is stricken dead.

Tristan de Pestivien, that squire of stature high,

By blow from Bélifort's rude mawle is wounded grievously.

Sore hurt is Rousselot, the brave.　And I may not deny

The Bretons have the worst.—Saints, to their succour fly !

VIII.

Fierce does the conflict rage, loud do the blows resound ;

Caron de Bosdegas, senseless, is on the ground.

And brave De Pestivien, who all-disabled lies,

On Beaumanoir for aid thus dolorously cries :

" Help me, good Baron, help me straight ; if I be captive

　　　ta'en

By these infuriate Englishmen, thou'lt see me ne'er again."

IX.

Then Beaumanoir he sware by Christ, who on the tree was

　　　tied,

Ere that should be, full many a shield and hawberk should be

　　　tried !

Hereon he flung his spear aside, and out his good sword drew ;

And all who came within its range he quickly overthrew.

But by his deeds the Englishmen were in no wise dismayed ;

And lion hearts on either side, the combatants displayed.

Wearied, at length, with such great toil, they on a truce
    agreed,
And for a while repose they took, whereof all stood in need.
With good wine of Anjou full soon their thirst they did allay,
And, thus refreshed, the deadly strife they recommenced straight-
    way.

Fytte ye Third.

Yet more of the same Combat; how Sir Robert Bembrough was

slain: and of the shrewd device of Guillaume de Montauban,

whereby the Bretons gained the Day.

I.

AGAIN the conflict rages fierce—again blows loud resound,

And splintered spears and battered helms bestrew the blood-

    stained ground.

The Bretons have the worst of it—it may not be gainsaid,

For two of them are slain outright, and three are prisoners made;

Thus twenty-five alone are left.   Christ Jesu lend them aid!

Then Geoffroy de La Roche, an esquire of high degree,

Knighthood besought from Beaumanoir upon his bended knee.

Whereon the Baron dubbed him straight, and thus said heartily:

" My fair, sweet son, spare not thyself, but emulate the knight,

Thy valiant sire, Budes de La Roche, who at Stamboul did fight.

Swear, and may Mary Mother be gracious unto thee!

That, ere the hour of complines, our foes shall worsted be!"

These words bold Bembrough overheard, and seeking how to

flout

The noble Breton chivalry, he scornfully cried out :

"Render thyself quick, Beaumanoir, and I will promise thee

Thy life, for I design thee as a present to my *mie*,

For I have vowed before her, and my vow I will not break,

That thee this night unto her bower I will as captive take."

Then grimly answered Beaumanoir, "I'll do as much by thee;

Thy gory head I'll send this night as a bauble to my *mie*.

The die is cast, and thou must stand the hazard; if it be

Against thee, by Saint Yves thy soul shall from thy body flee !"

II.

Now Bembrough's taunts had roused the ire of rough De Keren-

rais,

And thrusting toward the English chief he fiercely thus did

say :

" Presumptuous traitor, dost thou deem that thou canst captive
take

A noble knight like Beaumanoir thy mistress sport to make.

Beshrew thee !—never more thy tongue shall utter jape and jeer.

On this he smote him 'twixt the eyes with the sharp point of his
spear,

Right to the brain the steel did pierce as after did appear.[1]

Albeit wounded mortally, Sir Robert yet regained

His feet, and would with Kerenrais brief conflict have maintained;

But that Du Bois, discerning him, like lightning towards him sped

And smote him with his spear so hard, that down he fell stark
dead.

" Ho ! Beaumanoir !" Du Bois cried out, " behold thy haughty foe

Upon the ground, like a slaughtered hound, doth breathless lie and
low !"

When this he heard, the Baron good made answer joyfully :

" The time is come when we must needs double our energy;

Return ye to the fray at once, and let this dead man be."

---

[1] Que par my le visage, sy que chacun l'a veu,
Jusques en la cervele lui a le fer embatu.

III.

Meanwhile, the English men-of-arms, they all of them have seen

What sore mischance befallen hath their boastful chief, I ween.

When brave Croquart, the Almayn, thus to animate them strives.

"Too true it is—alack! too true—no longer Bembrough lives.

His magic books by Merlin writ, in which he put his faith,

Have played him false, since they could not forewarn him of his

    death.

But though our leader we have lost, yet be ye of good cheer,

Do as I counsel ye, brave sirs, and ye have nought to fear.

Keep close together, back to back,—keep close, betide what may;

And all who venture on attack, ye so shall maim or slay.

Heavens! how 'twill anger Beaumanoir, if he shall lose the day."

IV.

Hereon arose De Bosdegas, and brave Yves Charruel,

And Tristan, who was hurt full sore,—as erstwhile I did tell.

To Bembrough, when he captured them, parole they gave all three,

But Bembrough being slain, ye wot, they from parole were free.

Their shields they dressed, their swords they gat, then to the fray

    did hie,

Burning for vengeance on their foes, vowing they all should die.

v.

Now though the hardy English chief, bold Bembrough he is
gone,

Still furiously as heretofore, the conflict rages on.

Great smiting is there of their swords, great splintering of spears,

And their broad shields in cantels fly, while blood their harness
smears.

Natheless, the English yet can count full many a stalwart knight,

Whose strength and prowess doubtful make the issue of the fight.

Croquart the dauntless, Bélifort that knight of giant mould,—

Who, like a toy within his grasp, his ponderous mawle doth
hold,[1]—

Both these are left; and left also is Hugh de Calverley,

---

[1] Grose, in his Treatise on Ancient Armour, makes mention of Bélifort's
formidable weapon, calling it "a *leaden* mallet, weighing twenty-five
pounds." The writer of the Lay, however, is particular upon the point,
for he says:

> "Tommelin Belifort qui moult sçut de renart,
> Cil combatoit d'un mail qui pesoit bien le quart
> De cent livres *d'achier*."

And again:

> " Et Thomas Belifort y fu comme guéant,
> Cil combatoit d'un *mail d'achier* qui fu pesant."

With crafty Knolles, and many more.—And thus they fiercely cry,

" Vengeance for Bembrough we will have—spare none ! but hew

them down—

And victory shall crown our arms, ere yet the sun go down."

VI.

But Beaumanoir, who never did at face of peril quail,

Seeing the English stand aloof, would closely them assail.

And then began a strife so dread, that one incessant clang

Of weighty blows on helm and shield far o'er the wide moor

rang.

Already two brave Englishmen and an Almayn stout are

slain ;

Geoffroy Poulard in death doth sleep, and near him lies Dardaine.

E'en Beaumanoir himself is hurt.—Be pity on them ta'en !

Or not a man on either side shall e'er draw sword again.

VII.

But fiercely yet the fight doth rage—loudly the blows resound—

With streams of mingled blood and sweat blusheth the trampled

ground.[1]

—

[1] De sueur et de sanc la terre rosoya.

The day is passing hot, I ween—for the sun in heaven doth
    blaze,

And the combatants are bathed in sweat beneath his burning
    rays.

Now pious Beaumanoir that day had fasted rigorously,—

'Twas Mid-Lent vigil, and such fasts he kept religiously—

And being faint and sore athirst, for water he did cry.

Hearing the cry, Geoffroy Du Bois in accents stern did say,

" Drink thy own blood, De Beaumanoir, thy thirst 'twill quench
    straightway."[1]

Roused by these words of rough rebuke, and full of wrath and
    pain,

The Baron good forgot his thirst, and joined the fray again.

VIII.

Within a bowshot of the Oak, where grow the genists green,[2]

Like iron wall, immovable, the English band is seen.

---

[1] *Beaumanoir, bois ton sang!* became afterwards the war-cry of the
family.

[2] *Le lonc dun genestay qui estoit vert et bel.*

There Calverley ye may discern, the hardy jovencel,[1]

Gigantic Bélifort also, armed with his dire martel.

When Beaumanoir he found it vain to break their firm array,

Had not Saint Michael lent him aid he must have felt dis-

may.

But brave Du Bois, who near him stood, and saw his visage

fall,

Essayed by cheerful look and speech his stout heart to recal.

"Look around you, gentle Baron," quoth Du Bois, "and you

will see

That the bravest and the best are left of all your company.

Tinténiac, Yves Charruel, and Robin Raguenel,

With De La Marche abide as yet, and Olivier Arrel.

De Rochefort he doth yonder stand—you may note his pen-

noncel.[2]

Weapons for service lack we not—spear, sword, and dagger

keen—

And hands to use them we have got, as our foes know well, I

ween."

---

[1] Carualay, le vaillant, le hardy jovencel.

[2] The small, swallow-tailed flag attached to the lance of a knight.

IX.

Terrific is the conflict now—ne'er hath been seen the like!—

Incessantly the welkin rings with the great blows they strike.

The Bretons hurl against their foes; but moveless as a rock,

The English phalanx firm withstands the fury of the shock.[1]

Guillaume de Montauban hereon, that brave and subtle squire,

Seeing how matters stood with them, did from the press retire.

His breast swelled high with secret hope, and loudly he cried out,

That if a charger he could get, he would the English rout.

[1] In the edition of the "*Combat des Trente*," printed by M. Crapelet in 1827, from the manuscript in the Bibliothèque Royale, occur the following remarks in reference to the disposition of the English in the conflict. "It was within a hair's breadth that the position taken by the English did not procure them the honour of the day. The ardour and impetuosity of the Bretons would have been soon exhausted against this wall of iron; and tired of striking, after their first attack, they would themselves have fallen under the blows of their enemies. It is thus, that in the hapless days of Crécy and Poitiers, the sang-froid and discipline of the English troops triumphed over the number and valour of the French armies; in the same manner that at Fontenoy a column of English infantry sustained the shock of all the French regiments that came in succession to break themselves against its immovable mass; until at last, impaired by the artillery, it was forced into retreat, which it effected by falling back, always close serried, and in good order. History thus offers the most useful lessons of every kind, which, too often, remain without fruit for the people."

Sharp-rowelled spurs he fastened on, . then horsed him quick,
    I wist,
And a great iron-headed spear he took within his fist.
Yet toward the English rode he not, but semblance made to fly.

Astomed mightily and wrath, De Beaumanoir did cry,
" Whither so fast, De Montauban ?—what art thou, friend, about ?
Is it by flying from the field that thou thy foes wouldst rout °
Turn thee for very shame, false squire !" The other loud laughed
    out,
" Mind thy own business, Beaumanoir, and certes thou shalt find
As thou art frank and valiant knight, my business well I'll mind.

Then rowel-deep the spurs he plunged into his charger's flanks,
And wheeling round with lightning speed dashed towards the
    English ranks.
With the first shock seven doughty foes—yea, seven !—were
    overturn'd ;
And other three he trampled down, as quickly he returned.

By this great stroke De Montauban the English phalanx broke-
Into disorder threw them all, and their high courage shook.

Each Breton knight, as pleased him then, a captive straightway

    took.

And while the prisoners gave parole, De Montauban did cry,

" Now is the time !—strike, Barons brave ! Montjoie and victory !

Tinténiac, Yves Charruel, and Guy de Rochefort brave,

Strike all of ye with double force, and conquest ye shall have.

Christ Jesus in his clemency avert from you all ill !

And help you on these Englishmen to work your vengeful will."

X.

Yet still the conflict is not o'er, but rages fiercely on.

'Midst those who fought with Beaumanoir Tinténiac best hath

    done,

And on this memorable day hath palm of valour won.

But few upon the English side the combat now sustain,

For some are captives on parole, and others have been slain.

Sir Robert Knolles and Calverley are in great jeopardy,

And so is giant Bélifort, despite his bravery.

Vainly they struggle on.—'Tis o'er with every squire and knight

Who came that day in company with Bembrough to the fight.

John Plesington, Helcoq, Repefort, and Richard de La Lande,

With more to Josselin now are ta'en by Beaumanoir's command.

XI.

Oft shall they of this famous fight, in after times, hear tell,

For all its matchless feats of arms remembered are right well.

Pictured they are in castle-hall on gorgeous tapestry,

And sung in ditties of our old Armoric chivalry.

Full many a squire and hardy knight shall the stirring tale relate,

Full many a dame of beauty bright shall it serve to recreate.

And all shall glow as when they read of Guillaume D'Aquitaine,[1]

Of Arthur and of Oliver, Roland and Charlemagne.

Three hundred years hereafter—nay, a thousand !—they shall hear

Of this Combat of the Thirty, which, I ween, was without peer.

[1] Guillaume, Duke of Aquitaine, named also *de Gellone*, flourished in the time of Charlemagne, and was beloved by that prince, who employed him usefully against the Saracens. His deeds of arms form the subject of a romance, or rather warlike song, composed towards the end of the ninth century, or the beginning of the tenth, under the title of *Roman de Guillaume au court nez.*"—*Biog. Universelle.*

L'Enboy.

GREAT was the battle, doubt it not, and great the change it
  wrought.

Shame on those envious Englishmen—shame and defeat it brought,

Who Brittany, before that day, to subjugate had thought.

Now to Jesu, born of Mary, let us reverently pray,

That, by His intercession, all those valiant foemen may

Compassion find from pitying Heaven upon the Judgment Day!

May Saint Michael and Saint Gabriel plead for them with the
  Lord,

That to their souls at that dread hour his grace He may accord!

*Here endeth the Battle of Thirty Englishmen and Thirty
Bretons, which took place in Brittany in the year of
Grace, One Thousand Three Hundred and Fifty, on
the Saturday before* Lætare Jerusalem.

THE END.

LITERATURE.

Walton and Cotton's Complete Angler. With Original
Memoirs and Notes. By Sir HARRIS NICOLAS. In Two
Splendid Volumes, super royal 8vo. beautifully printed on
toned paper, and Illustrated with 61 exquisite Engravings
from Drawings by Stothard, Inskipp, and others. Handsomely bound in cloth, £2 2s.

This is, without doubt, the most beautifully illustrated edition of "Honest
Izaak's" charming Pastoral ever published. To the late tasteful publisher,
Mr. Pickering, its production was literally a labour of love. Neither time nor
expense was spared to render it worthy of the Arts and the importance of the
subject, and the result was a union of literary and artistic talent which has
rarely been equalled, and never surpassed.

Walton and Cotton's Complete Angler. Reprinted from
the Edition of 1676, with Extensive Notes and Addi
tions by "Ephemera," writer on Angling subjects in
Bell's Life. With many Illustrations. Crown, 8vo. cloth,
2s. 6d.

The Spectator. By ADDISON, STEELE, and others.
Revised edition, finely printed, 4 vols. crown 8vo. cloth, 14s. ;
or the 4 vols. bound in 2 vols., Roxburghe, 12s.

The Spectator. By ADDISON, STEELE, and others.
Complete in One Volume. Post 8vo. cloth, 3s. 6d.

Sterne's Works; including *Tristram Shandy, A Sen-
timental Journey,* &c. With a Portrait. 8vo. cloth,
3s. 6d.

The Complete Works of Oliver Goldsmith. Comprising
his Essays, Plays, Poems, Letters from a Citizen of the World,
Vicar of Wakefield, &c. With a Memoir. Crown 8vo.
cloth, 3s. 6d.

Disraeli's Curiosities of Literature. With a beautiful
Portrait of the Author, and a well-prepared Index by Dr.
Nuttall. Crown 8vo. cloth. price 3s. 6d.

Familiar Quotations: Being an Attempt to trace to
their source Passages and Phrases in Common Use. By
JOHN BARTLETT. Crown 8vo. cloth, 3s. 6d.

The great number of Quotations contained in the book has
created the necessity for a very copious INDEX, the
largest perhaps ever given in a similar Collection.

Liverpool to St. Louis. By the Rev. NEWMAN HALL, LL.B. Crown 8vo. cloth, 5s.

Notes of a Four Months' Journey in America.

Ourselves: Essays on Women. By E. LYNN LINTON. Crown 8vo. cloth. 5s.

"We women get rather hard knocks in these latter times."

Characteristics of Women. By Mrs. JAMESON. With a Steel Frontispiece. A Delineation of 23 of the Female Characters in Shakespeare's Plays. Characters of Intellect —of Passion and Imagination—of the Affections—of History. Post 8vo. cloth, gilt edges, 5s.

Three Hundred Æsop's Fables. Literally translated from the Greek. By the Rev. G. FYLER TOWNSEND, M.A. With 114 Illustrations designed by Harrison Weir, beautifully printed on toned paper by Clay. Crown 8vo. cloth, 5s.

Pleasures of My Old Age. From the French of EMILE SOUVESTRE. Post 8vo. cloth, gilt edges, 5s.

Naomi; or, The Last Days of Jerusalem. By Mrs. WEBB. With Steel Plates. Post 8vo. cloth, gilt edges, 7s. 6d.

What Men have said about Woman: A Collection of Choice Thoughts, compiled and arranged by HENRY SOUTHGATE, with Illustrations by J. D. WATSON. Crown 8vo. cloth, 5s.

The Language of Flowers. By the Rev. ROBERT TYAS. With 12 pages of Coloured Plates by Kronheim. 8vo. cloth, gilt edges, 7s. 6d.

The Standard Book of Etiquette.

Mixing in Society. A Complete Manual of Manners. By the Right Hon. the COUNTESS OF ————. Printed most elegantly by Clay. Fcap. 8vo. cloth, 5s.

"Manners make the man."

———o———